Running Fiercely Toward a High Thin Sound

Judith Katz

Ann Arbor

Bywater Books

Copyright © 1992 and 2017 Judith Katz

Print ISBN: 978-1-61294-107-3

Bywater Books First Edition: September 2017

Running Towards a High Thin Sound was originally published in 1992 by Firebrand Books, Ithaca NY

Earlier versions of this book appeared in the following periodicals and books: *Evergreen Chronicles, Hurricane Alice, Memories and Visions* (Crossing Press), *Sinister Wisdom,* and *Stiller's Pond* (New Rivers Press).

Printed in the United States of America on acid-free paper.

Cover designer: Ann McMan, TreeHouse Studio

Bywater Books
PO Box 3671
Ann Arbor MI 48106-3671
www.bywaterbooks.com

This novel is a work of fiction.

For Karen, Patty, and Paula, who held the mirror first.

Introduction

The 25th Anniversary of
Running Fiercely Toward a High Thin Sound

Twenty-five years ago, when this book was written, there had once been a town in Western Massachusetts with a large and growing lesbian population. There was a feminist film collective, a feminist bookstore, a collectively owned and run women's restaurant, a mostly lesbian-populated rooming house, and a few miles away in two directions lesbian-owned women's land. A course of study at the state university that is now known as some version of Women, Sexuality and Gender Studies was then known simply as Women's Studies. In the bigger universe there had been women's recording companies, women's music festivals, a half-dozen dedicated feminist and lesbian-feminist publishers, theater companies, little magazines, news rags, literary reviews, and filmmakers. The Stonewall Riots had incited a movement by then and ACT UP was clearing the path for AIDS activism. Ellen DeGeneres was not yet out as a lesbian—when she took that step she would call herself gay—and we would have to wait another twenty-five or so years for Jill Soloway's *Transparent* to make its way to what we now call television and delight and disturb us with all kinds of queer and Jewish family brilliance.

Back then, the terms *cisgender, gender non-binary, gender-fluid* and *gender-queer* were just a twinkle in some graduate student's parent's eye. We women who were attracted to and slept with other women called ourselves *lesbians*, and, much to the consternation of women similarly inclined who were a generation older than us, *dykes*. There was often considerable misgiving—read judgment—among middle-class white women my age around women who named themselves *butch* and *femme*. Drag queens were viewed with suspicion, and transgender was seen by the general public as a medical term, not a political one. This was a period when lesbians, coupled or single, were choosing to have babies by turkey baster or otherwise, and while some women were joining together in ritualized ceremonies, not only was the idea of state-sanctioned same sex marriage a different gleam in some future legal eagle's smarty pants eye, it was spurned as an attachment to patriarchal values by many of us because, as Joni Mitchell put it in her cisgender song, *My Old Man*: "We don't need no piece of paper from the city hall . . ."

So this book reflects the language of the time in which it was written—fifteen years ago an irritated cisgender male student of mine once went through and actually *counted* the number of times the word "lesbian" appears in this book. The central plot of *Running Fiercely Toward a High Thin Sound* clearly reflects the fact that in 1992 marriage was a privilege "enjoyed" by heterosexuals where a certain type of lesbian might be considered held captive by the expectation that she participate in the ritual as a bridesmaid. At the same time, another type of lesbian might feel outraged and wounded to be left out of the ritual and cause the kind of trouble the bride's sister Nadine makes when she is left out (kept out?) of the wedding altogether.

Who knew that just a few years later so many of us would be *able* to get that piece of paper from the city hall, and enjoy the celebration and legal protections that go with it?

When I finished writing this book in the early 1990s, Sarah Schulman's *The Sophie Horowitz Story* had been out in the universe for eleven years; and Elana Dykewomon's *Riverfinger Women* for twenty. By the time Nancy K. Bereano published the original edition of *Running Fiercely Toward a High Thin Sound* in 1992, that brilliant, farsighted publisher had made sure that works by visionary activist-artists such as Audre Lorde, Jewelle Gomez, Dorothy Allison, Alison Bechdel, and Leslie Feinberg among so many others had seen the light of day. Work by Jewish lesbians appeared in anthologies such as *Nice Jewish Girls* (Evelyn Torton Beck, editor) and *The Tribe of Dina* (Melanie Kaye/Kantrowitz and Irena Klepfisz, editors). Lesbian poets, Jewish and otherwise, for whom the personal was absolutely political such as Klepfisz, Lourde, Judy Grahn, Gloria Anzaldua, Cherrie Moraga, and Adrienne Rich found homes in both mainstream and small presses. It was a rich and glorious time in feminist and lesbian publishing.

And then, what Bereano called "rapacious capitalism" reared its head, and for a number of years small press publishing of any stripe and independent book selling became extremely difficult. Hopefully, some graduate student in some gender-fluid journalism program not too far in the future will write their master's thesis on what happened to small press publishing and independent book stores between the late 1990s and early 2000s at the hands of mega bookselling and publishing operations, which stole the market and some of the authors. Yet now, some years later, thanks in part to e-publishing, self-publishing, and determined small press folks like the women of Bywater Books, other thriving independent publishers, and bookstore owners who refused to give up, we stole the market back.

So twenty-five years later, what is this book? This book is a 1970s Jewish dyke's reflection on the town she came out in, and the family she grew up in—fictionalized, of course. It is a riff on the work of well-known Jewish storytellers like I.B. Singer, his brother I.J., Anzia Yezierska, and especially the beloved creator of the town of Chelm where all men are fools, Sholem Aleichem.

I wrote this book at a time when work by lesbian writers was nurtured and exploding into a welcoming and thriving culture. With that in mind, I invite you to imagine me, the writer, twenty-five years ago, sitting at my computer in a T-shirt and a pair of well-worn overalls, high tops on my feet, wild hairs flying in all directions, blasting Joan Armatrading and the Klezmer Conservatory Band on the stereo, as I made this story of one Jewish lesbian who never really left home and another, her sister Nadine, who was forced to flee.

Mostly I invite you to enjoy.

Judith Katz
Minneapolis, MN
July 2017

Running Fiercely
Toward a High Thin Sound

Prologue

The Amazing Human Torch

In the beginning was the fire, *ha esh*, which burned in my sister Nadine Pagan's eyes, then lit up like a burning bush around her head and took with it most of her hair. It spoke to us like God spoke unto Moses. In a high thin voice it sputtered, *Your sister is a lunatic, your middle child has gone mad.* For who else but a crazy person would steal the *Shabbes* candles from off the kitchen table and with them light her own head on fire? Who else would run as she ran through our house, shrieking like a blue jay until my mother caught her by the arm. "You *dybbuk!*" she screamed at the top of her mother lungs, and shook my sister as if she could put her out like some match.

Around in circles my father spun, first in one direction, then another, pulling at his chin as if he wore a beard. "What to do what to do what to do," he muttered, and still Nadine burned from the hair down until I myself came running and screaming, and poured water on her head, dumped it out of a waste basket until she was quiet and the fire in her head went out.

We all of us stopped and stared. The house smelled like someone had burned at the stake. Nadine's eyes were huge and hot. She did not cry, neither did she shout. We stared at her, and she stared back. For the first time since I could remember, the house was absolutely quiet. Suddenly my mother took matters into her

7

own hands. "You want something to cry about, how's this?" she shouted. She slapped Nadine first on one cheek and then the other. "It's not enough to set yourself on fire like a Buddhist nun, you had to do it with my grandmother's candlesticks, and on *Shabbes*! Whoever heard of such a thing?"

My father looked deep into Nadine's hot face. "See how you've upset your mother!"

I couldn't stand it any longer. "Nadine just tried to burn herself up! Call a doctor! Get an ambulance!" The words stuck in my throat like mud.

My father spun toward the telephone.

"Sure, call a doctor," my mother spat. "Call the hospital and a million psychiatrists. While you're at it, call the fire department, too. This is your older sister Nadine, Jane. Take a good look at her. She's a real beaut."

It wasn't the first time Nadine ever exploded, but it certainly was the most graphic. Ever since Grandma Minnie gave her that violin, Nadine and my mother rubbed against each other and made dangerous sparks. I believe Nadine's problem is inherited insanity. My sister Electa is not scientific, so she doesn't agree. Why aren't I crazy then, she argues, why aren't you? Electa wasn't there when Nadine lit herself up. She can only imagine it.

When Electa returned from the library that night the whole house smelled like burning flesh. All the windows were open even though it was thirty degrees outside. I was sitting in a corner of the living room crying. My mother paced back and forth in the kitchen and talked to herself.

"Where's Dad? Where's Nadine?"

"Ask your sister."

Electa stared at me. I stared back. "They're at the hospital."

"Is someone sick?"

"You could say that," our mother answered from the kitchen. We could hear her foot tapping.

Electa pulled the story out of us, sentence fragment by sentence fragment. "It makes perfect sense," she said.

"It was clearly the act of an insane person, Electa. How could it make perfect sense?"

"Well it does!" Even though Electa always left the house before things escalated to tonight's level, she fully understood the drama played out in our mother's house. Besides, our Grandmother Minnie had this violin.

Our Grandmother Minnie had this violin. It belonged to her father, our Great-Grandfather Yitzhach, who carried it with him on his lap to America all the way from Poland. He treated that violin better than he treated his own kids, that's what Minnie told us.

When he got to Ellis Island the customs officers made our great grandpa take his violin out of the case to make sure it was really a violin. This was, after all, a time of American gangsters with Jewish last names. Our great-grandpa obliged, but then the customs men wanted to break the violin open to see if he was smuggling anything inside. "Any one with two eyes can see we don't have a pot to pee in," *Zaideh* Yitzhach told them, but the guards insisted. Our *zaideh* refused.

Before they could snatch it out of his hands, *Zaideh* Yitzhach put the violin up to his chin and played. In the middle of our tired, our poor, our huddled masses yearning to be free, our great-grandpa played a Yiddish lullaby. For a fleeting moment, perhaps the only one in its history, all of Ellis Island was quiet but for the sweet, sad music he made.

Needless to say, the violin stayed intact. The people in line behind *Zaideh* Yitzhach applauded enthusiastically, then all became chaos again. My great-grandfather was declared a musical genius by two customs guards and his brother-in-law Tutsik. He collected his wife and five children. Tutsik found my great-aunt and their children, and together they boarded a train for New England.

In their new home, my *zaideh* played violin for weddings and bar *mitzvahs*. He also taught his oldest daughter, my Grandmother Minnie, to play. She was a good student, and when she learned enough, she gave lessons to the neighbor children and earned extra money for the family. She met her husband, Grandpa Irving, when he brought his little brother to learn from her. He brought her a piece of fruit from the family store at each visit, and over weeks, months, then years, Irving courted Minnie with apples, bananas, oranges from Florida, until finally they wed.

By then Irving had his own store, and he and Minnie lived above it with their children—in chronological order, my Aunt Miriam, my Uncles Davey and Mike, and my mother, Fay. Irving ran the store and Minnie gave lessons and between them they made a decent living and their children did well in the world.

But Fay, my mother, was unhappy. She saw my grandmother teaching all the neighbor children to play the violin. She admired the cases they carried and the delicate instruments within, and she longed to play as they did, as her mother did, on *Zaideh* Yitzhach's violin.

Grandma Minnie, however, refused to teach her.

"I didn't refuse. I saved her from grief. Simply put, your mother had no talent. I knew this from the day she was born. Her hands were all wrong. Why frustrate her? I only told her I didn't have time."

Whether or not my mother had talent, what was nature and what nurture, this we will leave for the psychologists among us to decide. The fact of the matter was that every time a neighbor child came for Minnie's lessons, my mother fumed inside. She was a good girl and never complained. Instead she bore her rage silently. It dropped anchor inside her. It grew and spread like a fungus. From time to time it leaked out my mother's eyes.

In the meantime, my Aunt Miriam taught my mother to play the piano. Fay was competent, but she lacked inspiration. It was the smooth wood and catgut, the bow in her hand that kindled my mother's imagination. The cool touch of ivory under her fingers did nothing to fire her up. What passion she might have let loose on a violin became detached technique when she sat at the piano.

Time passed.

My mother Fay met my father Mel. She was buying shoes at his family's store. He was impressed with the turn of her ankle and the fact that she spoke intelligently on several subjects. She was enamored of his soft-spokenness and the gentility with which he slipped her foot, with the aid of a shoehorn, into his latest styles.

"Your mother was a regular Cinderella to my Prince Charming" my father used to tell us when we were small. "Can't you girls see it even now?"

Mel knew Fay, and they begot Electa and then Nadine and then me, the youngest sister, Jane. Electa and I had moderately happy childhoods. Nadine was silent and far away from the day she was born. Even though her face wasn't scarred until after she set herself on fire, it seems to me that that purple ring had always been there. Electa and I played with the neighbor children, we read, jumped rope, and went to the movies. Nadine sat and stared, with that wild look in her eye, out the window, into the woods behind our house, up at the moon and stars.

All of us visited Grandma Minnie, but it was only Nadine who was allowed to play her violin. "Of course I let her play it. She has a gift. I knew it the minute I touched her tiny hands. That girl will win prizes, I said. I knew what I was talking about."

So while Electa and I ferreted through Minnie's closets for fancy dresses and costume jewelry from another time, Nadine sat in the living room, plucking and pulling at the strings on *Zaideh* Yitzhach's violin.

One year for my mother's birthday, Minnie made a big party. She cooked the whole dinner herself and invited all of us over, and my Aunt Miriam and her husband Al, and even the families of Uncles Davey and Mike, who traveled to us from Boston and Hartford. The meal was delicious: vegetable soup, baked fishes, kugel, and sour cream. For dessert we ate honey cake and strudels. The grown-ups had brandy with their tea.

After dinner we all sat in the living room and gave my mother presents. I gave her earrings I picked out myself. My uncles gave

11

her a sweater, Miriam gave her a skirt to match, my father gave her a bracelet with many colored stones in it and signed the card, *With love from me and your three jewels*. When the gifts were passed around and the wrapping paper folded up or thrown away, my grandmother cleared her throat and clapped her hands. "Now Nadine and I have a special gift for you, Fay. I taught her the tune, but it is her own ability which gives what will follow the magic I know you will all perceive." With that, Grandma Minnie nodded her head and Nadine left the room. When she came back, Nadine stood before us all and tucked the violin under her chin.

"And now," said Minnie, "a birthday *frailech*." She waved her hand, and Nadine began to play.

And what music! For three generations and four families time stood still. Though a *frailech* is a happy tune, by the time my sister Nadine was done there was not a dry eye in the house. When she first finished there was complete and stunned silence. Then my uncles and aunts hooted and clapped. They stomped their feet, they pinched Nadine's cheeks. "A prodigy!" Uncle Dave declared. "Ought to be on Ed Sullivan," said my Aunt Miriam. "What do you say, Fay, aren't you proud of your daughter?"

All eyes, including Nadine's, which smoldered, were on my mother, who sat with her arms crossed in front of her, tapping one foot. Her lips were pursed, her eyes narrow.

"Who taught you how to do that?"

"I taught her," my grandmother said.

"You taught her but you wouldn't teach me?"

"That was years ago."

"But you wouldn't teach me."

"The girl has a gift!"

"And me, I have nothing, isn't that true, *Mameh*?"

"I wouldn't go so far as that—"

"Happy birthday," my mother muttered as she walked out of the room. "Happy birthday to me!"

After that there was no peace between my mother and my sister Nadine. Minnie gave Nadine the violin to bring home. The secret was out now: Nadine had a talent, she needed to practice. But the fact of the matter is, when the violin came home with Nadine that day, my mother went mad.

Whenever Nadine practiced, my mother always found a reason she should stop. Either she must clean the bathroom or wash the dishes or vacuum the carpets first, even after Electa or I had done that work ourselves. Or sometimes when she began to play my mother developed sudden migraine headaches and Nadine must stop, she must, the music made my mother's pain too great.

When Nadine did chores as she was told, my mother complained that the job wasn't done well enough. When Nadine ignored her and continued to play, my mother nagged at her until she had no choice but to stop. My mother whispered at night to my father that Nadine was torturing her on purpose, deliberately trying to give her headaches. She paced about the house and muttered just under her breath that Nadine was a rotten child with no respect for a mother's aches and pains. According to my mother, Nadine was rebellious and callous. She was selfish, had no consideration. How would she like to be in pain and have violin music played in her face all the time, *hmmm hmmm hmmm*?

Soon the violin went back to Grandma Minnie's. Nadine was to practice it there. But this did not make my mother happier. Now she complained that Nadine was never home. "You like that violin of yours more than you like me. You care more about your grandmother than me, your own mother. Well, get this through your head, sister—your grandmother will die soon and you'll have me to contend with for another forty years. You better get used to it. One mother is all you get."

Eventually Nadine stopped practicing altogether, and her life became pure hell. My mother shifted her displeasure from the way Nadine did chores to the way she looked. Her clothes needed mending or else ironing or else my mother told her they were out of date. Even when Nadine managed to get her clothes looking just the way she thought my mother liked them, a new shoe dropped: No matter what Nadine did, no matter how she combed it, tied it, or tucked it behind her ears, my mother always hated my sister's hair.

I cannot name the exact day it started, but one autumn morning when Nadine was fourteen, she began to rebel. "Your hair looks like a rat's nest," my mother told her. "Go comb it."

Instead of leaping from the kitchen table as she usually did, Nadine stuck a piece of bread into the toaster and waited for it to pop. "I said go comb your hair." Electa and I looked at each other across the jam and butter. My father poked his head out from behind his newspaper. The toast came up cheerlessly. "Did you hear your mother?" my father asked.

Nadine picked the toast out and began to butter it.

"You heard your mother, now what are you going to do about it?"

Nadine smiled at my father and began to chew. For a few minutes there was no sound around the kitchen table except for the crunching of toast and the nervous clatter of Electa's and my silverware against our breakfast plates.

"She smiles!" my mother finally boomed. "If you think I'm going to let you out of the house looking like that, you've got another thing coming!"

I looked at Electa and Electa looked at me. Compared to some of the girls we knew, Nadine's hair looked like it was set in a beauty parlor.

"What's wrong with it?" Electa ventured.

"Wrong? Look at it—it looks like a swamp full of leaves!" My mother grabbed Nadine away from the table. "I'll show you to contradict me!"

Into the bedroom they went, my mother wielding a comb. She pulled it through my sister's hair as if she were raking the lawn. When she was done, my mother came back to the kitchen rubbing her hands, triumphant. "Nadine!" she shouted over her shoulder, "hurry up, you'll be late for school."

Nadine crept in with her coat on. Her shoulders were up around her ears. The edges of her hair were smoothed down, but her eyes were red from crying. "There, doesn't she look much better?"

Neither Electa nor I said a word. From that day on, I'm not sure Nadine spoke either. At meals her head was always bowed. She glared when anyone spoke to her. Still my mother kept on about her hair, which she had recently taken to wearing in a tight ponytail. The more my mother picked, the darker Nadine's eyes grew, the more silent she became. She stooped when she walked and spent hours in the basement doing only God knew what. Electa thought maybe she was developing mass murder plans. "You watch, Jane, she's going to explode one day and kill us all, wait and see."

I didn't want to wait. I went down in the basement myself to see if I could find any knives or axes. Instead I found a long, thin board nailed to a cigar box. Beside them I found music notebooks filled with Nadine's own compositions. The notes inside them were wild and complex. But how could she hear them if she played plain wood? It reminded me of deaf Beethoven. Suddenly she came up behind me and whispered, "Put them down, Janie. They're mine. Put those notebooks down."

"How do you hear the music?" I asked, gingerly handing them back to her.

"It's in my head," she whispered, and with a bony finger poked at her temple again and again.

Electa and I made up this story. One day when I was just a baby in the carriage, Electa took me for a stroll across the park to Grandma Minnie's house. We hadn't gone far when a naked girl, half human, half wolf, covered with dirt and mud, came up to the carriage. Her hair was matted, and she smelled terrible, but we could tell from the way she whined and whinnied that she wanted to be our friend. So we took her with us to Grandma Minnie, who bathed her and clothed her and took the snarls out of Nadine's hair. When she was groomed and well-kempt, we brought her home to our parents.

"Please, please, let us keep her!" we begged.

"I don't know. Is she a nice girl?" my mother asked.

"We'll train her, we'll teach her!" my sister and I swore.

My father looked at my mother and she back at him.

"Well, if you promise," my father said in a sweet, fatherly voice.

"We do, we do!"

"She does seem awfully nice," my mother said.

"Yes, you can keep her," said my father. So without further ado, they adopted Nadine, who has been part of our family ever since.

And it came to pass after the fire that my sister Nadine spent many days and many nights in the psychiatric ward of the hospital. She had the best help for disturbed adolescents our money could buy. She had a private room, and that room had a window that looked out onto some woods below.

My sister Electa went away to college, and my mother was asked by doctors not to visit Nadine at first, so the only company she had besides her psychiatrist and the nurses was my father and me.

I came to her by bus. Always I found her, head in hands, staring out into the woods. I brought her tapes of music by famous violinists. We listened to them together, and fat, slow tears slid down Nadine's cheeks. They slipped into the gully of her purple scar, then down her gritty neck. For the longest time, Nadine did not speak. She only glared and grunted. I wrote her notes and handed her paper and pencils to write back, but she ripped the papers up and broke the pencils in two. I began to think that she truly had become the wolf girl Electa and I imagined so many years before. Even though she scared me I made sure I went to see her at least three times a week.

My mother sent presents with me or my father. Cookies she baked herself, a new nightgown, a box of candy. My father, when he went, always brought flowers. He appeared in her doorway like a reluctant suitor and pretended to knock. Then he pulled a plastic chair up close to the bed and the two of them stared at each other sadly.

One month passed, then two. Nadine's hair began to grow, but her purple scar did not fade. Her voice was full of gravel when she spoke. Once or twice when my father came to visit, she smiled.

One day the psychiatrist and my father came to see Nadine together. "The word is," my father said, "you might be ready for a visit from your mother. What do you say?"

Nadine looked at my father with animal eyes.

"It will be a short visit, Nadine. Your mother is very eager to see you."

Nadine's eyes traveled from psychiatrist to father and back to psychiatrist.

"She'll come with your father the day after tomorrow."

Nadine nodded her head, then turned on her music and stared out the window some more.

When my mother arrived, she was laden with gifts. Nadine sat on her bed and looked at the packages. Then she looked up at my mother. "Don't you want to open them? I brought them for you."

Nadine turned her head toward the woods in the window. My mother, taking this simply as a sign of catatonia, reached out to touch Nadine's new curls. "Your hair is coming in nicely," was all she said.

"Oh, you like my hair?" The ragged edge of my sister's monster voice confused my mother. She jumped back as if slapped.

"I only wanted to tell you how pretty you look."

"I have a mark around my face! I look like I have been in a train wreck. My voice sounds like a cement mixer. How can you call me pretty!"

"Nadine, please, you're upsetting your mother."

"Look, Nadine, at all I have brought you."

"Sweet things. Frilly nightgowns. Who cares? Look at me! Hear my voice!"

My mother was livid. "Ingrate!" She slapped Nadine.

Nadine's nostrils flared. "You can do that at home but you can't do it here. I am a sick person in the hospital. Don't try that here!"

"Is this my daughter? How can it be? Listen to her voice, Mel. My daughter doesn't sound like that. There's a *dybbuk* inside her! Just listen!"

"There's no *dybbuk*, Fay. This is America in the twentieth century. That is really your daughter who said those things. She is mentally ill."

"That's right. I'm nuts. Look into my eyes!"

"You can't talk to me like that!"

"I can," Nadine growled, "I am a patient. I am under doctor's care. I can do whatever I want. I can tell you anything. Now I want you to GET OUT OF MY ROOM!"

There was silence. My mother stepped back from her daughter, my father pulled his invisible beard.

"Your room?" my mother hissed. "Who do you think is paying for this room? Who hired the doctors? Who wants to find you a good plastic surgeon so that some day, if all is well, you can look normal?"

"I WILL NEVER LOOK NORMAL. GET OUT OF MY ROOM!"

"*Vildeh chei-eh!* Wild animal! This is some gratitude for everything we've done." Then without a word my mother descended upon Nadine and began to hit her with both her fists.

My father rushed out of the room and came back with an orderly who gathered up my mother and escorted her out. "You don't understand," my mother told the young man as he helped her with her coat, "she's my own daughter but she doesn't respect me."

"It's a shame," said my father, who followed closely behind.

In time Nadine was released from the hospital and my parents had to figure out what to do with her. At first she lived in our house, but none of us could manage it. We couldn't get her to look at anyone but me, no matter what we did. Nadine sat like a cat at the living room window and stared out all day long, or she looked down at the floor in front of her or at her plate on the kitchen table. She was falling deeper and deeper into herself, to where, no one knew.

Finally my Grandma Minnie offered to take her in. This irked my mother no end, but even she agreed it was for the best. "At least she'll be able to practice that *farbrocheneh* violin there without driving the rest of us crazy. Who knows? My mother is such a hotshot in the kitchen, Nadine might even finish her dinner once in a while and God forbid help with the dishes."

So we packed her a bag and took Nadine to live with my grandmother. There she thrived, although she still hardly spoke. For it was not only the scar around Nadine's face that was destined to stay forever, but also her strange, strangled voice. This was further proof of my mother's theory that a *dybbuk* was lodged inside Nadine. I, her New World daughter, assumed with my sister Electa that fifteen years of silent screaming finally let loose in Nadine's throat and tore her vocal chords to shreds.

She didn't really need to talk anyway. From the time she woke up in the morning until she went to sleep at night, my sister Nadine played her violin. My grandmother coached her, but in a year Nadine outdistanced her. "There's not another thing I can do for you," Minnie told her, hands in the air.

There was talk of Julliard and other fancy conservatories, music scholarships, awards for emerging artists, but Nadine would have none of it. The fact of that purple scar around her Jewish face was also problematic, but Nadine refused plastic surgery. Besides, her voice was so awful, how could she talk to other musicians and patrons of the arts dressed in fancy gowns and tuxedos? She didn't want to be the famous mute concert violinist. She wanted to be an extraordinary musician in her own right, for her own pleasure and no other.

My grandmother heard Nadine's arguments, shrugged her shoulders, and tapped her foot. "If that's what you want out of life, go in health, *zei gezunt!*"

Not many weeks later, that is exactly what my sister Nadine Pagan did. Into a knapsack she put two pairs of underpants, an extra sweatshirt, her toothbrush, her music notebooks, and loose change she scavenged from all of the pockets in all of her pants. Then she gathered up our Great Grandpa Yitzhach's precious violin, put on her sturdiest shoes, and walked out the back door of my grandmother's house into the darkest summer night.

Part 1

Chapter 1

History Lessons

You were the new dyke in town, Nadine. Me, Rose Shapiro, I brought you there myself. In my own arms with my own hands, although at the time I was myself under water, the underwater life I made by rolling sticky green pot between thin sheets of paper and smoking it like some grade-B movie lesbirado. But I remember your arrival as if it happened yesterday. The story goes like this.

I was driving back from Cambridge at three in the morning with a pound of homegrown Vermont sinsemilla which I purchased from my friends Verna and Leslie in order to sell it to the dykes of New Chelm to help get them high and also pay my rent. I sampled the pot and sampled it some more and by the time I finally picked my smoky way out of Boston, I had given up all hope of ever seeing the Mass. Pike or any of my girlfriends in New Chelm again. So you can imagine my relief when I finally saw a sign that said Route 9 and remembered from my frequent trips back and forth across the state for purposes of buying high-grade lesbonic weed for the good of the people that if I followed it west, Route 9 would take me all the way into the tiny town of my home, New Chelm.

One look at any map will show that an inevitability of Route 9 is the city of Worcester, of which I can say not one good thing. Except, that is where I found the hero of our story, the aforementioned—you, Nadine Pagan.

On that night, Nadine, you looked like a wolf if ever I saw one. You stood with your thumb out under a street light in a flannel shirt, jeans, and high-tops, your wild hairs tied back to make you look like a boy, but I wasn't fooled. Years of looking at women in moonlight showed your true self to me. I pulled over and pushed open the door of my little bug and into it you slid.

You are a small woman, but there was a heaviness to you then, Nadine. Not a heft, but a great weight that seemed to be lodged firmly on your slight shoulders. You wore a knapsack and carried a violin case which you put carefully on your lap like some baby. Then you bundled my twisted seat belt around you both and stared straight ahead.

"Where are you going?" I asked. I was tempted to give you a lecture about the dangers of middle-of-the-night hitchhiking for women, but here I was with a Volkswagen full of marijuana, stoned out of my mind, so really, who was I to talk?

You turned your face to me, and there in the street lamp light I saw it, that big purple ring around your face that was your face. I gulped a little because it was awesome and I reached my fingers to touch it but stopped short because—did you flinch? Did you duck? Did I remember that I was a lesbian and were you one or not? How could I know? Instead I put a hand on the steering wheel of my little yellow bug, let out the clutch, and we were on our way into the woods that stretched between dreaded Worcester and home.

"I don't care where you are going," you said in a voice that sounded like fingernails running down a chalkboard. "I have nothing to lose."

I twisted the radio dial this way and that until I found something that sounded like music. The pickings were slim as it was far into the middle of the night and we were in Worcester after all. But now, with you my companion, it became a fine night to travel. I rolled down the window on my side and realized I knew this road and, better yet, how to get off it and on to a more magical one. And so, with a flip of my blinker and a turn of my wheel, we began to sail through the beautiful and curving roads that brought us from Worcester to Ware to Belchertown, New Salem and points west, with rises and falls, dips and turns, until finally we crossed the concrete bridge that carried us over the Chelm River into the New Chelm Valley and up the rickety alley of a street that was the center of town.

"This is where the journey ends," I told you. "I live down that street over there. Do you have a place to stay?"

You unlocked your seat belt and gathered your violin to you. You looked with your ringed face into my own and leaned toward me. Then, with a fierce glint in your eye, you kissed me on the mouth. Oh, Nadine, I was yours from that minute on.

The love we made was animal. Biting, chewing, untrimmed fingernail sex, sex that scratched and pulled me in the wrong places, but how could I say no? These were the early days of public lesbian life. No one was even sure if they knew the right way to go down on someone, let alone talk about it or ask for it a different way. We had sore cunt sex at its most enjoyable, the kind I thought about two days later and my cunt clenched, my knees got weak, and I couldn't wait to be biting and sucking and chewing you again.

I know now I was your first woman lover but I couldn't tell that then. I was marveling because your enthusiasm and clumsiness were no different than that of the other six women I'd been with so far. What was different was your passion, Nadine, which was wider and stretched me further than any of my other lovers. And a sorrow that I sensed just under your snarly surface, a sadness so vast it begged me to jump into it and soothe you. I wanted you more than any of those other women, who were sweet enough and smart enough but never quite poked at my heart the way you did. You were so far away so much of the time, Nadine, but I viewed you then as I view you now—my first and truest love.

How did you manage to come out while you were living with your grandmother or with such a dark scar etched into your crazy face? Did you plod through the card catalogues in the Worcester Public Library to find books about lesbians, homosexuality, inversion, and deviance? Did you wolf around the one gay bar in Worcester to find others like you? I still don't know, and in those days I never thought to ask.

I just figured based on how you kissed me that you always had and always would be a lesbian like all the other dykes I knew by then. Before you came around I was kind of a big shot, one of the famous New Chelm lezzies who came out in an undergraduate clump over at the University. I was in charge of refreshments, provided lovely weed and exotic trips that came on squares of blotter paper, tools to make the dancing easy. Those were the days! How we rubbed each others' backs and got crazy jealous and high. How we horrified ourselves by tossing our ex-lovers' keys down the sewer right before their eyes, or sleeping with someone one night and then not speaking to them for months, maybe years after. How we marveled in the taste and pull and differences in each others' spicy cunts.

By the time I brought you to my bed, Nadine, I was already part of the five-year dyke club. Had my own room in the New Chelm lesbian rooming house on Vick Street, my own collection of lesbian tracts and theories, and a dozen posters on my walls, all artifacts of our new-forming lesbo archeology. Dated and lovely ornaments of our earliest struggles to locate not only others like us, but even ourselves.

I never questioned your credentials, Nadine. The fact of your landing your mouth on mine just an hour after I met you was proof enough of your queerness for me.

I got you a room down the hall from my own in the Vick Street house. To call it a room is generous. It was in fact a gable with enough floor space to contain the thin piece of foam that was your bed, your music stand, and the world's tiniest desk. You kept your clothes rolled up in balls and tangles in the cubby that passed for a closet. It was lucky you had hardly any possessions and no one to visit but me.

In those days, as you know, I supplemented my pot-selling

income by working as a prep cook and cashier at New Chelm's dyke restaurant, *Lechem V'Shalom*, a Hebrew name that translated into Bread and Peace—in any language, two necessities of life. It was an enjoyable job which met all my social needs. Through those doors, six days a week, practically every dyke in the world came for herb teas or soups full of the vegetables I chopped with my own two hands, eggs over easy, potato *latkes*, black beans and rice, or any of the other delicacies of vegetarianism we collectively rotating cooks might provide.

You took a job as dishwasher at *Lechem V'Shalom*, first for free meals and then for the small check that paid your rent (twenty-seven dollars a week) and provided some extra for the necessities of your life, which included, among other things, tampons, violin strings, paper, and pens.

It was hard work to get you that job, bottom of the lesbian pile though it was. Because your voice was tightly strung you hardly spoke, and some women thought you mute. Because your wild hairs flew out from every side of your purple scar with a Health Department-regulated *babushka* tied around your head, some suspected you were berserk. The scar itself made you monstrous to some, and for these reasons you were relegated to the back of the restaurant with the garbage and cracked plates. It was months before you proved yourself sane enough to wield a knife against carrots and onions, green beans and tomatoes, in the society of our kitchen.

Yet through this all, you seemed almost cheerful. You slept into the morning, wandered the streets of New Chelm for exercise, then went back to your little room and played on your violin for hours and hours until it was time to make your way to the back door of the restaurant. You ate your dinner, then paid it off by spraying down dishes and shoving them into the washer. Then you came out to the back stoop to smoke a hand-rolled (tobacco) cigarette with me, emptied the clean dishes, and started all over again.

We hardly spoke at the end of those nights, but still, I loved you better than all my other girlfriends. As we strolled back up to

Vick Street, a lit joint passing between us, there were times when for no reason at all you started to laugh like the maniac most of New Chelm feared you to be. But that didn't bother me, Nadine. I loved how we'd holler up to the top floor of the rooming house because neither of us remembered our key. Before long, some dyke or other in a flannel shirt and a pair of overalls, with hardly any hair and a crabby disposition, came to let us in. When together, usually in giggles, we made our way up the creaky stairs and into my bed, we had more sore cunt sex, more laughing and howling, until one or both of us fell asleep. I was determined to let my other lovers go. I dreamed of a life with you alone, Nadine, the two of us ragged outlaws against the rest of the whole sad world.

Chapter 2
Acts Of God

After Nadine left my grandmother's house with the *slap slap* of Grandma Minnie's screen door, there was a short calm. Then, as if Nadine had set not only her own head on fire but all of ours as well, my mother began to scream and would not stop screaming. Any time she spoke to me or my father, what should have been a simple exchange of words turned into gun shots and bottles flying. The mere act of saying hello might become flying daggers of swear words or, even worse, no words at all. And always, deep into the night there was my mother's incessant mumbling and my father's circular pacing. Between the two of them, I wondered if I had not died and ended up in hell.

Enter my sister Electa, her last year of college, confident and charming, law school acceptance letters streaming behind her like peacock feathers. Her boyfriend Mickey would have kissed the ground she walked on if he thought Electa's feet ever touched it. When they came to our house together, their visits were sporadic breaths of savior air. If she had never come to see us, I surely would have died or been killed.

It was Electa who coached me toward college, who sat at the kitchen table with my sunken parents and stuck it to them about Nadine's disappearance.

"Have you called the police?" she would ask.

"Please, Electa," my mother answered in monotone, "the police to find an eighteen-year-old runaway? We know she isn't dead."

I wasn't so sure. My mind ran to the sorry facts of modern life. Headless women found in trash heaps, little girls turned into whores, drug addicts, and underground terrorists. " Why don't you call?" I mumbled. "Because, Jane," came my father's measured tones, "in the first place she's legally an adult. If she wants to go, it's a free country. What good could it do?"

What my father was secretly thinking he never said, but I could hear it as loudly as if he had burst out with it like my mother always did. If Nadine wanted to bite the feeble hands that fed her, that was her business. Good riddance to her. If she didn't want the plastic surgery they'd offered while she was still at my grandma's, fine. He'd use the money to send me to college. If she chose not to contact us, to disappear into the night and possibly be murdered by a stranger, whose fault was that? Not ours, certainly.

But if that was the case, why did my mother sit at the kitchen table night after night blaming herself as she read news and obituaries, combing the paper for clues, such as missing fingers, found teeth, decomposed clothing, and other hints that might lead to some logical explanation of the disappearance of her daughter Nadine.

I prayed for Electa to save us totally, but she did not. When September came she packed her car and her boyfriend and off they went to the middle of the country to study law together. They disappeared over the horizon to their own safety, and I was left alone with a mother who would not budge from the same place on the couch and a father who barely returned to us from work at the shoe store at day's end.

I, Jane, was left alone to finish the work of my life, which at the time was high school, and also to do, as best I could, the work of maintaining my mother and our house—the kitchen work, the dusting and mopping, and always responding to her calls. Jane help me with this and Jane help me with that, Jane hold me up and Jane lay me down.

I was utterly abandoned to my mother's wide and specific despair.

Then, at last a miracle. A fat letter came from the state university accepting me into their enormous student body. How joyously I fled, although admittedly not without guilt, not to Chicago which harbored Electa, or even to Boston, where I might be consumed by flashy big city life, but just an hour and a half away to the Chelm Valley, the little city in the middle of nowhere, to the university with a capital U where all was possible and my zombified mother was only eighty miles away. Close enough to call and coddle over the telephone and far enough away so that I might explore the new and marvelous science of women's studies and with it the most fabulous of feminist side effects, the possibility of a life with women who stood up for themselves, who took care of each other and fought with each other, and most delicious and terrifying of all, sometimes took each other to bed.

My mother grew restless in her empty house. Not entirely empty, because late at night, maybe not so late, eight or eight-thirty, nine-thirty or ten, my father eventually returned from the shoe store. Shopworn and weary, he ate what my mother cooked for him. She ran on energy she stored while sleeping on the couch for much of the day, awakening around five in the afternoon to prepare fabulous dinners—steak and baked potatoes, or fish in creamy sauces, complemented by leafy green vegetables which my father pushed around on his plate like a little boy. He chewed and stared into space while my mother tried at small talk. Did he want more salt? she asked. Ketchup? she wondered. What condiments and taste enhancers for their fast-fading appetites could she possibly provide?

For three years I came home from college twice a month for *Shabbes* dinners sporting a lesbian persona which grew thicker with each visit. Both parents seemed too dead in the eye to notice my overalls, my increasing wardrobe of T- and flannel shirts, although my father, shoe man that he is, did notice my thick-soled orange work boots and came momentarily to life.

"What are you now, a mason? I thought you were pre-med." He reached down and poked at the end of my foot. "Waddaya got in there, steel toe?"

My mother continued her walking dead waitress act, placing plate after plate of *Shabbes* food before us.

"Those shoes are for men," he continued. "They're bad for your feet. Girls come into the store and want them, I send them elsewhere."

When my mother sat down, my father concentrated on his dinner. There was no sound but the scraping of spoons in bowls, the cheerless slurping and munching of food that I normally thought delicious, except I was eating it with the dead and could barely taste it. My life at the university was alive with politics and romance. Home was a graveyard, but the main body, my sister Nadine's, was nowhere to be found.

I didn't dare bring it up.

Finally, one *Shabbes* dinner was not like the others. My grandmother was there, which didn't surprise me. She was usually at dinner when I came home. My father picked her up at the nursing home and brought her over like a strange sabbath date. The odd thing was that also at dinner were Electa and Mickey who had flown in all the way from Chicago, and Mickey's parents, Sima and Dave, and no one had mentioned it to me beforehand. They were all dressed up for a special occasion. I was in my by now well-worn overalls, so I spent a great deal of time trying to make myself disappear.

There was a bottle of first-rate champagne on the table and a group of fancy long-stemmed glasses in a clump next to it. Something monumental was up, and I wasn't wearing the right clothes for it. It was a conspiracy. "Don't you ever wear anything else, Jane?" my mother asked as she fidgeted over the chicken. She brought it to the table and set it down right in front of my father. "Didn't you tell her, Electa, that this was a celebration?" She shook her head, surveyed Sima, Mickey, Dave, my grandmother. Under her breath she muttered, "I hope there's going to be enough to eat."

"You always cook enough for six armies, Fay. Of course there's enough. Besides, once everyone hears Electa's news they'll all be so happy they'll forget about food."

"What are you, Electa, pregnant?" my grandmother asked. Mickey's mother looked horrified.

"Please, Ma," my mother snapped.

Mickey pulled himself up in his seat and adjusted his tie.

My mother looked from him in his sports coat to me in my overalls. The whole time I knew Mickey he had never dressed like that. I felt betrayed. I was also very glad that I didn't bring my girlfriend Kria along with me like I'd thought about doing. I had a picture in my head of us pulling up to my parents' house on her motorcycle, me swinging off it like some cowboy, presenting Kria to all. "This is my current lover," I would say, and she would wipe her hands on her jeans, brush back her short hair with her left hand, and offer my father her right one. "Nice to meet you, Mel," she would say. Then she would punch my mother in the arm in that jocular way she had. "You must be Fay," she'd say, and that would finally wake my mother up enough to notice me again.

My mother plunked a bowl of green beans and another of mashed potatoes onto the center of the table like sacrificial offerings.

"Can we get on with it already? Dinner is on the table."

"Sit down, Fay, for godsakes. Let's do this civilized."

Mickey's father and mother cleared their throats and shifted a little in their seats while my father opened the champagne and poured it with great ceremony into each of our glasses. My mother finally sat down, but she didn't sit still. "The food is getting cold."

Dutifully I reached over and put some green beans on my plate. Electa slapped my hand. "Hang on, Jane. Daddy is making an announcement."

"Announcement nothing," my father said, "this is a toast." He stood up and the entire contents of the table, including the *Shabbes* candles, shook. Mickey's parents pretended not to notice.

"You're shaking the table, Melkie," my grandmother scolded.

My mother sighed and rolled her eyes. She slipped my overalls another disapproving look.

My father took a little sip of champagne and looked out at all of us officiously. I mentally prepared myself to hear the Gettysburg Address. "Why is this night different from all other nights?" my father asked, looking with great meaning into each of our faces, "because on this night, our beloved Electa Yael is going to reveal a delicious secret. As the father of Electa Yael Morningstar, I am honored—more than honored, thrilled—that she chose *me* to inform you all of a momentous journey she and her young man, Mickey Robbins, have chosen to embark upon—"

At the words *young* and *man* Mickey gulped. My mother in the meantime looked significantly at the chicken on the table which was admittedly losing steam.

"Oh, Daddy, I didn't mean for you to make such a big deal about it. Mickey and I are getting married, that's all." My father looked at Electa and then into his wine glass and finally sat down. The table shook again.

"So, *le'chayim*," he said, I thought a little dejectedly, and forced a smile at his future in-laws and my mother. You could tell he had a big speech prepared and that once again the women of the house had wrecked his moment.

"*Le'chayim!*" my grandmother cried." *Mazel tov, mazel tov,* Mickey, you're getting away with murder!" That was her way of telling him he was a lowly (although good-looking) *shlub* and didn't deserve my sister, the queen of law school.

Suddenly my mother leapt to her feet. Everyone except Mickey's parents held their breath. What was she going to do? "Isn't it wonderful!" my mother shouted. "Electa, you've made me so happy!" She threw her arms around my sister and we all breathed a sigh of relief. For the first time in years a light came into my mother's eye, as if, perhaps, she might regain her will to live.

And then something horrible happened. Electa looked me right in the eye and said, "And Jane, Mickey and I want you to be the maid of honor."

"What do you say, kid?" Mickey winked at me. At least he didn't call me Princess.

"Of course, she will," my mother answered for me, and like a trained seal, I nodded my head and agreed. At that moment I became two people: the Real Jane, politically active and astute lesbian, who could stand up to patriarchal authority in all of its forms without batting an eye, and the Good Daughter Jane, Barbie doll monster, who went through all the motions of preparing to sell her oldest sister up the river for an electric dishwasher and a toaster oven.

I didn't realize the depths to which I plunged until Kria came over for supper the next night and I had to tell her I'd agreed to be the maid of honor. I blurted the whole thing out just before we went to bed. Kria stared at me blankly, pulled off her heavy black boots, and sat at the edge of my bed. We had only been sleeping together for a couple of months and already I was engaging in reactionary political behavior. I had no idea how she was going to take this news. I was a nervous wreck. I threw my head back cavalierly and said, "Don't you think that's funny?"

"That they asked you to be the maid of honor? Did you say yes?"

Indeed. How could I have said no? Even if my mother had not accepted for me, who else would do it if I did not? What other sister was available to dress up in a funny costume and stand by Electa while she promised to love, honor, and put the toilet seat down for Mickey until the day they both died? Besides, my mother had finally come back to life. How could I jeopardize that?

"You gonna wear lipstick and high heels and a girdle?"

"What else am I gonna wear? Overalls?"

"Hmm," Kria said. We exchanged a perfunctory kiss, and she fell asleep immediately.

I sat up in the dark with my eyes wide. When I finally slept I dreamed I was dancing in a gay bar with Emma Goldman. "Is it the lipstick and the girdle Kria objects to?" I asked as Emma whirled me around in a jitterbug turn. "Oh no," replied Emma, "it's the wedding itself." Then she let go my hand and went twirling away with Audre Lorde.

I woke from this dream with a start. It was the first of many such dreams featuring well-known feminists like Adrienne Rich, Angela Davis, and the Grimké sisters. Each helped explain the ways in which being a bridesmaid supported the oppressive institution of heterosexual marriage, but all of them evaporated before I could get them to tell me how to get out of my duties.

Over breakfast the next morning Kria's brown eyes flashed as she lectured me on the ways in which I was giving my energy to an opulent, overpriced spectacle that symbolized everything we had been working to topple.

"But it's my sister's wedding—a Jewish wedding—"

"All the more reason to resist," Kria said. "Think what a big impression you'll make if you refuse to put up with it."

"What can I do about it? I agreed to be a bridesmaid. Does that make me a traitor?"

Kria buttered her toast and smiled at me sweetly. She didn't have to say anything. I was a traitor, not just to Kria, but on a more general level to all lesbians of all races and classes everywhere who were more likely to be shot on the spot than celebrated if *they* were to announce an engagement and send parchment invitations like the one I was to receive to everyone they ever knew, including their grandmothers, cousins, and best friends from grammar school.

And what about my sister, Nadine, who was missing in action but part of the family after all?

Chapter 3
Double Vision

In time, Nadine, you became a regular part of the scenery at *Lechem V'Shalom* women's restaurant in scenic downtown New Chelm. By regular I mean that over the years the collective had stopped relegating you to back room p's and q's and now displayed you and your scarred face proudly, right out in front. There you took money and orders, poured coffee, made toast, and once in a while, when things were astrologically just exactly right, laughed at people's jokes and made what sounded like conversation.

Nadine Pagan is how we came to know you in New Chelm. Even I, who over those passing five years still periodically shared your bed and coaxed you toward unbelievable noises in the middle of the night, had no idea what your other last name ever was. I called you Pagan because you fit into no laws I understood. That seemed to please you for a private reason all your own, and so Pagan became your name and you became a fixture at *Lechem V'Shalom*, a point of civic pride.

It was you who was often the first person any woman saw when she traveled from far away to the only all-women restaurant in western Massachusetts. You became a sentinel, the one who never asked, "Can I help you?" but always did. As lesbian legends go, you were famous, at least to other lesbians, and we thought that everyone knew you existed and who you were.

Not exactly who you were. The thing about you, Nadine, is that you came to us with no family, and so we all assumed you never had one. No wonder everyone was a little startled when your original roots made themselves evident. Not nearly as startled as you, which surprised us, since we assumed you knew you had a family all along.

The evidence that you had a life before New Chelm surfaced on a steamy spring morning—steamy temperaturewise, and sexwise, since it was that part of spring when everybody had already broken up with their old girlfriends and were melding into hot *new* couples joined at the wrists, hips, and lips. It was one of those late-spring Sunday mornings when every lover and her ex-lover and her ex-lover's grandmother was walking through *Lechem V'Shalom's* door to show herself off. Not only was I working my butt off to keep those breakfasts coming, I was bummed out, because like I said, you and I were still sleeping together every now and then, but every time we did, especially if the sex was really good, you stopped talking to me.

I had by now given up all my other lovers, including Crystal who worked at the collective with us, which made things less than comfortable. I really missed you when you did a disappearing act, especially on days like today when I had to look at you all the time. You stood right at the front of the restaurant over by the toaster, a red *shmatteh* tied around your head, your wild hairs spilling out every which way. You wore a tight T-shirt and no bra, and shorts with an apron over all of that. Your hairy legs and work boots poked out under the apron, and you were sweating like crazy so your scar was really purple. You had this big bread knife in your hand and this demento dyke look on your face. This combined with the rock-em-sock-em-maybe-this-singer-is-a-lesbian music that was on the stereo, and I mean even I thought you looked berserk—although admittedly in a bucolic and very sexy kind of way.

You were an *artist*. You used to play that violin so sweet out in the back yard of the restaurant, in the dark, when business was slow. I loved when you went out there in warm weather, Nadine, and played that saddest music. It was a real treat because for once I could actually see you. Usually you played late into the night in your little hovel of a bedroom at the Vick Street house. There was always a group of us women hanging out in the hallway outside your closed door, listening and listening. Sometimes, Nadine, you played a song so beautiful that it drove us all to tears. Then we'd applaud outside your door, but nothing ever happened. You never came out and took a bow. You always played as if no one was listening, as if no one cared.

This is just a long way for me to tell you that scarred and strange or not, Nadine, you were a most valued member of our community. Sometimes you made everyone nervous, but we loved you just the same. Me, I loved you more than anyone.

But back to this particular steamy Sunday morning I was talking about. You were buzzed on coffee and in a pretty good mood. To tell you the truth, it made me sad to see you so happy because the night before I begged you to come over to my place and get high. You said no, and I ended up getting loaded by myself on these fabulosa lesbonic flower tops I scored from my Boston friends. So there I was, busy flipping cakes and also wondering just what it was that put you in such a good mood (and not feeling any too great about it either), when this miracle occurred.

The door of the restaurant swung open. The little bell above it rang like it always did. First this dyke from this one women's studies class I was taking over at the university walks in. A motorcycle politica named Kria. Boy, have we had some fights. She's one of those people who thinks it's totally wrong to get screwed up on drugs and keeps calling pot "the man's tool." Givez moi une break. She's really cute, too, which makes it all the more infuriating. You should see the muscles on that woman's arms!

Anyway, here it was so hot out and all, and this Kria comes in wearing a fucking black leather jacket. I couldn't believe it. She swings in like some cowgirl, and I think, oh great, Sunday morning, my favorite time for a political correction. But she doesn't come in with her guns on—she actually smiles at me. It looked like politics was the farthest thing from her mind. But that wasn't the miraculous part. The miraculous part was that right behind her came this Jewish dyke in a pair of overalls and a T-shirt who, except for the fact that her hair was a lot shorter and she was a little bit rounder, looked exactly like you, Nadine, only with no scar. I mean, really, you guys had almost the exact same face.

You looked up just at the minute they walked in the door and I took one look at your face and I thought, this is it, lesbian kills puffy double with bread knife. Details at eleven. The two of you saw each other and *kaboom*. It was the weirdest thing—two Nadines, one scarred, one smooth. You were like real Superman and Bizarro Superman, only it was real and Bizarro Nadine. I thought I was hallucinating, but no such luck. Everybody else noticed it too.

Real and Bizarro Nadine stared at each other like itchy cats. Then the real Nadine, you, hissed something. I couldn't catch what it was. Then Bizarro Nadine hissed back. Kria sauntered over to the wall and hung out there trying to look casual. Frankly, I was amazed she seemed so calm. I was a nervous wreck. Now that I think about it, Kria did look a bit green. Everybody looked green at that point. We were all wondering what was going to happen and nobody knew. I tried to act nonchalant, like none of this was making me nervous, but when I reached around to turn the music over I knocked a pitcher of water off the counter and had to move between you two Nadines to wipe it up and pick up the broken glass.

All at once, Nadine, you started laughing your head off. I mean you laughed and laughed and laughed and laughed and then, without saying a word, what do you do? You stop laughing and just walk into the kitchen. Of course I followed you. I watched totally mouth open as you slammed the refrigerator door so hard the pans rattled around you. Then you started tossing stuff into plastic containers and wrapping up leftovers which was really crazy because we were serving breakfast for another two hours. "Hold it," I said, "what's going on?" You stared at me for a second, then we heard the screen door slap shut once, twice. Then a motorcycle revved up and peeled out. Ever so slowly, little bubbles of conversation formed out front, and I could hear women rustle over their food again. Crystal or somebody put new music on the tape deck.

You picked up a kitchen knife and started chopping onions indiscriminately. Some one out front hollered, "She's gone!" A sickening high school kind of giggle drifted toward us. You kept chopping. I stood next to you and sucked my breath in. "You can put the knife down," I said, "they left."

You acted like you didn't hear me. I put my arm around your shoulders like I did during our earliest times together when I couldn't figure out how else to calm you down. You pushed my arm away and continued to chop. "Nadine, who is that woman?"

You looked at me like I was from Mars.

"Who is that woman?" you asked me back in your clearest voice to date. "My sister. My true sister."

41

Chapter 4

Secret Message

Me I smoke again, Jane, from the inside, but not from matches. I am burning up inside and laughing at the joke of it. Here you are all the time right across the river at the university and what about me? Here, I am here. Nobody calls to me in waking life, but every night I dream you Jane, and Electa, I dream her too. The two of you, my true sisters, I dream you. *Chop chop chop.* Watch the smoke rising. This is a sign. I am discovered. My cover is blown. In my dream there is a message. In my dream Electa is dancing in a fancy dress and you, Jane, you dance with her. In a circle, under a canopy of thorny branches, in one another's arms. I am atop the canopy, hidden in the moonlight, howling like a dog. Nobody hears me however loud I yell. Nobody hears me howling like a dog while around in a circle dances our mother in a gown of red taffeta, a big rose pinned to her bosom, how she dances around the canopy, she tosses rice at us and gasoline. Me, I bay and bay but nobody hears me. Around our mother in a circle dances our father back and forth, in a line, in place, in place. A balcony appears out of nowhere. Grandma Minnie stands on it wearing nothing at all. She tosses stick matches with heads aflame onto our canopy, fueled with gasoline and rice. Then I shout at the top of my voice, *Do you see me? Am I here now?* No one puts the fire out, but nobody burns either. Only me.

Chapter 5
Dyed-To-Match-Shoes

I rode home to my little apartment that Sunday on the back of Kria's bike. I held tight to her, but for the life of me I can't tell you how we got there. All I remember is getting on the bike and her dropping me off, then lying in my bed thinking, I have to call my parents. Only I didn't want to call my parents. How could I? My mother was just starting to wake up now that Electa was getting married. If I told her Nadine was living in New Chelm working in a restaurant she'd fall asleep all over again. Then there was the actual fact of Nadine. She looked like she had been baking in an oven for years. She looked absolutely insane.

I went out and bought a pack of Camel straights and then came back to my apartment and smoked them end to end. I kept staring at the telephone and smoking cigarettes. The ashtray got full. I dumped it and filled it up again.

What killed me was the way in which Nadine, who had been missing from my life for five years, just turned around and left me standing in that stupid restaurant in front of all those other lesbians with my mouth hanging open. It was only the third or fourth time I'd been out with Kria in public, and there we were in the middle of all of these women I went to school with. I was totally embarrassed.

I was also very disappointed. How was it that I didn't know

until that morning that Nadine was right over the river and that she was, from the look of things, a lesbian like me? Why had I never dreamed her so close to me or seen a sign? And instead of embracing me, holding me to her, the worst thing had happened: Nadine had recognized me and turned her back on me. Me, Jane, her sister. The sister who was always there with a bucket of water to put her out. It saddened and infuriated me.

Now it was up to me to decide whether or not to tell my parents I'd found her.

It wasn't exactly as if I never saw my family and could just ignore it all. I was to be Electa's maid of honor. Suddenly, after years of looking the other way when I entered a room, my mother was calling me all the time to remind me that I should start to lose weight and clear the acne off my face, to normalize, heterosexualize, or at least become neuter.

What was I supposed to do about Nadine, who lived right across the river chained to a stove and obviously did not want to see me? Was I duty-bound to visit or ignore her? Bring her the family news or bury it? I was of many minds not the least of which being that I wished for the first time she was as dead as I had imagined her.

Logically, I should have been able to discuss Nadine's reappearance with our sister Electa, but her impending wedding was turning Electa strange and I no longer saw her as my savior or friend. She and my mother were all of a sudden thick as thieves. I don't know why Electa didn't just let my mother be boss of the wedding and be done with it. While she was away at law school my mother was doing all the work. But then Electa came to spend the summer in Worcester so they could make *plans* and, I couldn't believe this, she set up a kind of headquarters in her old bedroom. Of her own free will she moved back into my mother's house and seemed to be enjoying herself.

Even though I had a summer job at school, I still had to be around the two of them a lot of the time and they drove me crazy. Weeks passed, and I didn't tell them I had seen Nadine. When I couldn't push it out of my mind, I felt extremely guilty.

I got a wedding invitation in the mail. Why didn't they save twenty cents and hand it to me some Friday night when I came to dinner? It was engraved in tiny copper script on pale brown paper. It said:

Melvin & Fay Morningstar
Request the Honor of Your Presence
At the Wedding of Their Daughter
ELECTA YAEL
to
MICHAEL ZACHARY ROBBINS
Son of
David & Sima Robbins
Ceremony to take place at Temple Beth Shalom
Saturday, August 14, 1978
R.S.V.P

There was also a little white card with more copper engraving that said, *M_____ will____ will not____ attend,* and a small stamped envelope on which my parents' address was hand printed. I read it over and over and over, then I sat down on the living room floor and I cried. I flipped the invitation over. There was a personal note to me, from Electa:

> *Jane—*
> *I'm glad you could see your way clear not only to attend*
> *but participate. We will be off on a bridesmaid's dress*
> *buying expedition next Saturday. Call with questions.*
> *Kisses,*
> *E.*

Bridesmaid's dress? Saturday? I had a date with Kria for an all day motorcycle trip into the country that Saturday. She was impatient enough with me already because I wouldn't go to the women's restaurant over in New Chelm again. "Why don't you want to talk to her? She's your own sister?" I never told her the whole story of Nadine setting her hair on fire or running away. I never told her about my catatonic mother. I just acted like it was no big deal and like, why should I go there, Nadine obviously didn't want to talk to me anyway.

The other thing was, Kria and I liked each other a lot, but we hardly had any time to see each other. Kria was committed to saving the entire world, not just the lesbians, and consequently she was very busy. She was on the board of the Chelm County battered women's shelter, the Committee to Combat Racism on Campus, and at least three other advisory panels. I was trying to study feminist ethics, biological sciences, and make time to do at least one political good work a week. Also, out of deference to my sister Electa, I agreed to spend at least two Friday nights a month with my family.

We'd been planning this trip into the country for a month. I agreed to take an entire Saturday off from studying, and Kria got out of two meetings. Now my sister and mother were planning an ad hoc buying spree. I called Electa right away.

"How's my favorite maid of honor?"

"I'm OK, Electa, but why I'm calling—"

"Not changing your mind are you? Jane, it will kill Mommy!"

No such luck, I wanted to say, Mommy's been a zombie for twenty years. Nothing will kill her. "No, I still plan to do it. I just can't come Saturday."

"Whatsa matter? You gotta work?"

"No, I have personal plans—"

"Jane honey, this is a personal plan—"

"I have a personal life and a personal plan that isn't about the wedding."

"You gotta date with a guy?"

"Not with a guy, no."

"With a girlfriend? Bring her along. It's going to be really stupid and tons of fun. Mommy promised to take us out to lunch after. I want to really do it right and go to one of those places where they cut the crust off your sandwich and bring you tea in a silver pot. Bring your girlfriend along. It'll be a riot."

"I don't think so, Electa." Somehow I couldn't see Kria all

decked out in her leathers and mirror sunglasses meandering through some bridal boutique. It also didn't seem like the right time to say, "Listen, Electa, I'm a lesbian and this so-called girlfriend is my lover and we have better things to do than stand around and discuss hosiery." So I didn't.

In fact, the list of things I decided it wouldn't be a good time to tell anybody was getting longer and longer. If I told them I was a lesbian, Electa would accuse me of sabotaging her wedding. If I told them I saw Nadine and I thought she was a lesbian too, I'd be dead. My family was a walking Greek tragedy, and my mother had lots of potential to shoot the messenger. Now I had to tell Kria that our romantic lesbian spree into the far reaches of lust in nature was off so I could go buy a uniform of the patriarchy.

"You can break up with me if you want to," I said, "I won't blame you or anything."

Kria said she was disappointed, but as it happened, there was an emergency budget meeting at the shelter and now she could make it. "But listen, Jane, I'd be careful if I were you. If your sister Electa is anything like that Nadine, I'd wear a bulletproof vest."

That was what was confusing. Electa wasn't anything like Nadine. She was normal and actually very cool. She was part of the first big wave of women law students in the country. She and Mickey were going to have hyphenated last names. But now, living at my mother's, Electa was turning into a movie star. She swung into rooms like she was wearing some pink chiffon dress with sunglasses and gloves all the time, and my mother was practically following her around with a clipboard like Della Street on "Perry Mason." She and my mother drooled over caterers' menus and sample invitations like a couple of teenagers looking at pictures of rock stars. My mother called every florist within a fifty-mile radius who made *chuppas*, and she and Electa gushed over color schemes, guest lists, and seating plans with so much enthusiasm it made me nauseous. Which was weird because Electa didn't usually care about any of that stuff and now she was playing into it like it was the most important thing in the world. More important than the

ERA, or the boat people, or any of the stuff she was going to law school to change.

All this I considered as I sat wedged between my mother and sister in the front seat of Electa's car several days later on our way to the bridesmaid gowns. While the two of them chatted about silver and crystal, *hors d'oeuvres*, and floral arrangements, I felt my lesbian self disappear into the car upholstery. My spirit was being absorbed by vinyl and foam rubber, so that by the time we arrived at the department store where I was to be fitted for my wedding costume, it was not the real me but the zombie Jane who walked between my mother and sister through the big glass doors.

My mother led the way confidently through sportswear and makeup, perfume and purses, to an elevator. She guided us certainly down a corridor filled with china and bric-a-brac, past a room full of headless torsos dressed in bras and girdles, into the bridal boutique, where we were greeted by mannequin after mannequin dressed in white, holding bouquets of paper and silk flowers, veiled, placid, smiling. This was my mother's territory, and she navigated like a pro.

A tiny woman in sturdy shoes found us among the silky gowns and greeted my mother and sister warmly. "Jane, this is Sarah," my mother told us with surprising animation. "Sarah, this is Janie, my other daughter. Of course you know our bride-to-be, Electa."

Sarah reached up and pinched my cheek. "So you're the maid of honor. Let me set you ladies up in dressing room three."

It took me a minute to remember they were talking about me, that I was the honor maiden. Nonetheless, when Sarah led us to a far corner of the bridal boutique, I followed. Sarah jingled a huge ring of keys and unlocked a white door. "You go in and make your-selves comfortable. Mimi will be in to fit you in a minute."

"It's lovely, isn't it?" my mother gestured broadly at the small private room. Mirrors covered three walls, a white shag rug was on the floor. The furniture was early Barbie doll—two plump white hassocks and a satin couch.

"I hope you have a decent bra on," my mother said as I unbuttoned my shirt. I suddenly couldn't remember if I had on any bra at all, but before I could pull my shirt back on the door swung open and there stood Mimi, who must have been Sarah's depressed twin. She had a tape measure around her neck, a long pink dress slung over one arm, and a pair of white linen pumps clutched between her thick fingers. Sighing deeply, Mimi hung the dress on a chrome hook and set the shoes down at my feet. Then she kneeled in front of me and with the help of a shoe horn slipped my foot into one of the pumps.

"Like a glove," Mimi said as she got me into the other shoe.

"I don't think I can walk." I stood and wobbled from one end of the dressing room to the other.

"A little practice, you'll be fine," my mother said.

"Besides, you'll kick them off as soon as the dancing starts."

I was surprised to hear my sister Electa's voice. She hadn't said a word since we got into the department store.

"She won't kick them off," my mother argued.

"I probably will," I answered, disturbed at the whine in my voice, " but still, I have to walk down the aisle—"

"Don't worry, Janie, we've got a nice strong best man for you to lean on when it comes to that." Electa winked conspiratorially.

Best man? I never even considered I'd have to wobble on some strange guy's arm on top of every other thing. "But I still have to stand up at the altar teetering—"

"For God's sake," burst my mother, "the heel is only a half inch—less than that. You can practice standing. It won't kill you—"

"I could break my neck," I said softly.

"Yes, think of the headlines," Electa said, "FEMINIST SISTER DIES IN TRAGIC HIGH HEEL ACCIDENT: 'I DIDN'T THINK IT COULD HAPPEN HERE' SAYS SHOCKED BRIDE."

"Alright, Electa, cut the comedy," my mother said. "Mimi, the shoes fit. Let's try the dress."

"*Oi*, the dress."

"It's not gonna kill you to wear a dress and heels and look like a *mentsh* for five hours."

"It totally contradicts my political world view."

"Stop talking nonsense. Mimi! The dress."

The dress was worse than I'd imagined. The sleeves were sheer, the bodice and hem frilly. I cringed at the thought of wearing it in public. "Electa, this is a real girly outfit."

"I know, Jane. I'm sorry, but it's the best of what they're offering this year."

"What's wrong with it?" my mother wanted to know. "A dress is for girls to wear. What were you expecting? Lace overalls?"

"It's just so—"

"Feminine?" my mother sneered. "Look, we haven't got all day. Try it on."

I slipped out of the rest of my clothes. To my relief, I had remembered to wear a bra and if it wasn't clean, my mother didn't notice. I climbed into the dress, which pinched at the waist as my mother zipped it.

"It's too small, Ma."

She pulled up at the zipper, and my sister Electa empathetically held her breath. Mimi the seamstress evilly fingered the pins in the cushion on her wrist.

"It really doesn't fit," I said weakly.

"It fits. With a different bra—you know, it wouldn't hurt to lose a few pounds before the wedding anyway . . . *oi* . . . there." My mother triumphantly slipped the zipper all the way shut. I saw myself in the three dressing room mirrors. I recognized the face, but I couldn't place the body anywhere. "Ma, if I turn purple because I can't breathe it's gonna spoil the effect."

"You only have to wear it once. It's fine."

"I'm gonna faint."

"Alright, we can let it out, can't we, Mimi? Jane, take it off."

Mimi unzipped, and I dutifully stepped out of the dress.

My mother snatched the dress out of Mimi's hands and carefully examined the seams. 'T here's plenty here to play with."

"Ma," Electa looked our mother in the eye, "let Jane try the next size."

"It will fit like a tent."

"Please, can we try the next size?" Electa asked the seamstress directly, by-passing my mother, taking matters into her own bride-to-be hands.

Mimi returned in a few minutes bearing another gown exactly like the first but bigger. I numbly climbed into it. It zipped like a charm but hung oddly in strange places.

"What did I tell you," my mother said triumphantly, "a tent."

Electa again went over my mother's head. "Mimi, what's easier? To take in or to let out?"

"In my professional opinion, it would be easier to find a style that fit the young lady to begin with."

A tear formed in the corner of my eye. Electa sat back in her chair with her head in her hands. "This is impossible. I can't find one dress that looks good on five different women!"

"Try the smaller size again."

"Ma, I can't fit in the smaller size."

"Can't means *won't."*

I stood looking at myself in the larger dress. I pressed my eyes in to hold back a fit of crying. Electa touched my shoulder. "Really, Jane, it's not so bad."

"The smaller one is better," my mother said flatly. "Jane, try the smaller one just one last time."

I stood paralyzed in the middle of the dressing room.

"Really," said my mother, "I just want to prove a point. Please step into this."

She held the dress open like an envelope. I looked at Electa who looked at Mimi who silently washed her hands of the entire matter. Then Mimi unzipped the bigger gown and held it while I carefully stepped out.

The other women held their breath as I wedged myself into the first dress. My mother once again tugged at the zipper.

"It's gonna rip."

My mother squeezed the flesh of my back in under the zipper and yanked. "I could use a little cooperation. Pull your tummy in."

"It's in as far as it will go."

"Mommy," Electa pulled herself up to her full height, which in the space of the dressing room was rather impressive. "I'm not going to watch you torture Jane one more minute. Jane, you put on the large dress. Mimi, you pin it."

My mother threw up her hands and sat in a corner where she sulked until the pinning was complete. Normally I would have been nervous that she was going to lapse into her depression again, but right now I had troubles of my own.

"It's not my fault I can't fit into a size-eleven dress."

"No comment," my mother muttered.

She was still alive, and I was an adolescent again. The fluorescent light made my skin green, my teeth yellow, my face puffy and full of tear streaks. I wobbled in my white linen pumps while Mimi took pin after pin from her pin cushion wrist watch, poked, adjusted, and sighed.

At last, the seamstress got up off her knees. She dusted her hands and opened them to my reflection in the mirror. "You look like a million," she said.

Even through the straight pins, I could see that the dress looked better, although it was nothing I would ever choose for myself.

I picked my way out of the dress. My mother said, "Don't scratch yours elf. If you get blood on that dress it's ruined."

I put my own clothes on but still could not recognize myself in the bridal boutique mirrors.

"You look exhausted," said my mother. "C'mon. I'm gonna buy you girls some lunch."

Kria wasn't angry with me as much as she was annoyed. We had so many urgent and pressing matters right where we lived, matters of survival. The money it took to buy a dress and a pair of shoes I could only wear once, the cash my family was spending on all the festivities, the stress and strain I was feeling trying to stuff my lesbian psyche into the most traditional heterosexual ritual in the world, seemed like a tremendous waste to her. And besides, I had given up a day of erotic motorcycling through the wilds of the Chelm Valley and the exciting sex that would follow.

So she didn't have much sympathy for me when I showed up at her place after my day of endless chatter and humiliation at the bridal boutique.

In all fairness, Kria did the best she could. She made me a beautiful dinner of green salad, brown rice, steamed tofu. She sat across from me at the dinner table and began to eat, I hoped, with an open mind. But as soon as I started rambling on about mirrors in the dressing room and the too-tight bridesmaid gown, the fluorescent lights and my mother's lose-twenty-pounds-before-the-wedding litany, Kria drifted to another land.

"Hello?" I said.

Kria pushed the lettuce around in her wooden bowl. She picked at it with chopsticks and then pushed the whole thing out of her way. "I hear you. I'm just thinking about my day, which I notice you haven't bothered to ask about."

I poked at my own lettuce and then pushed my salad bowl out of the way, too. "OK," I said, folding my hands, "tell me about your day."

"Well, since we canceled our date I got to go to the budget meeting for the shelter today."

I nodded politely. I wanted more rice but I kept hearing my mother counting the calories.

Kria got up to boil tea water. "In order to pay rent, salaries, and overhead for the next six months—and just the next six months—we've got to come up with fifteen thousand smackers. One of our biggest backers just cut her annual contribution in half. If we can't find that much in the next two weeks, East Chelm is out a battered women's shelter."

The kettle whistled. Kria pulled out two tea bags and stuck them in mugs. I rolled a leaf of lettuce up between my thumb and forefinger and smoked it like a cigar. "Why don't we tell my parents we want to get married? Then we can take all the money we'll get and save the shelter."

"You'd have to tell them you're a lesbian first, remember?" Kria rolled her eyes and tapped the kitchen table a little like my mother does when she's about to explode. "Your parents are spending more money on this wedding than most women who use the center will ever see in their lives. So what if you got forced to stand in a pair of stupid shoes in a posh little dressing room while your mother told you to lose weight. If we don't figure out a way to get funding there's a whole group of women of all different sexual orientations in New Chelm, South Chelm, and points east and west who aren't going to have anywhere to go when some boy beats the shit out of them—"

"Just because I'm going to be a bridesmaid at my sister's wedding?"

Kria stared out the window. I wanted to crawl under the kitchen table and stay there.

"I can't help it," I told her, "they're my family." There was that awful whine again.

I tried to get Kria to talk to me some more about something else, but it was useless. I cleared the table and helped with the dishes. Then without even kissing her good-bye, I walked out the door and went home.

Chapter 6
How I Found The Wedding

I find where you live, Jane. Just a little apartment in a tiny house across the river from New Chelm. The tiniest house and you live here alone I know because there is only your name on the mailbox. I know because there is only one tiny bed, I can see it through a window. The door is locked. I knock and rattle. I will enter through a window. I will break and enter into that window looking for you, Jane. Jane Jane Jane. You came to see me at the restaurant but I couldn't talk. Why should I? How could I? I looked at your face and no words came out but only laughing. What on earth could I say?

I pry open the window of the house of you, my sister Jane Morningstar. I hang now like orangutans I have seen in the zoo, outside the kitchen window, two hands at the top, two feet at the bottom, and drop down into your house through a window open just a crack. I drop feet first through the window and swing and swing and land on both feet in the tiny kitchen.

What do I find? A pile of dirty dishes in the sink. Three science textbooks stacked neatly under a filthy coffee mug. A pile of papers ranging in all directions. Five cigarette butts with no filters ground out in an ashtray.

On the refrigerator a picture of that woman you came with sitting on a motorcycle smiling. Is she your sweetie pie your honeybunch your girlfriend? My nostrils flare. I prowl into the bathroom and sniff out two toothbrushes, five hairs in the sink, a million hairs in your brush. I am looking for something what is it what is it what is it?

On my tiptoes I slip into your bedroom. Two ratty pillows on the bed. What's this, a vibrator? I push the switch down and it buzzes like a giant bug. Then *RING RING RING* three times, the telephone. I stand frozen, a catch in my breath, on the third ring a machine voice says, *Hi this is Jane. I'm not home now but if you leave a message . . .* and then another voice, stiff, more mechanical than the tape, *Hi Janie, this is Mom calling. I guess you already left so I'll see you in a little while. Just wanted to remind you to wear a decent bra. Talk to you soon.*

Mom? My Mom? Our Mom together? Why do you need a clean bra to see her? All of a sudden I have a funny feeling which I do not like. I drop down on all fours and snuffle along the walls of your room. How different it is from my own. Books on the shelves, books piled on the floor, what books, *Lesbian Nation, Patience and Sarah, Sisterhood Is Powerful, Women, Race and Class.* Do you read all of this at once? And listen to all of these albums and tapes? Where do you get it all? What do you do to get it? I have almost nothing, and you have all of it.

Suddenly I realize something horrible. Your rooms are full of old furniture from our mother and father: rocking chair, kitchen table, black and white TV. I kick the TV, I shove over a stack of books, and then there it is, an envelope with very fancy handwriting addressed to you, Jane, opened and handled. I pull it out and what do I find there? This is what I am looking for, here is the fact. What does it say? What does it say?

Melvin & Fay Morningstar Request the Honor of Your Presence At the Wedding of Their Daughter Electa Yael to Michael Zachary Robbins Son of David & Sima Robbins Ceremony to take place at Temple Beth Shalom Saturday, August 14, 1978 R.S.V.P. And a little white card with more copper engraving that says, *M_____ will_____ will not_____ attend*, and a small stamped envelope on which our parents' address is printed.

By hand. I read it over and over and over, and the note on the back of the invitation to you from Electa, the personal note, the note that shows absolutely that you are a member of the wedding and I am not. A bridesmaid. What am I then? Who am I? A nobody.

A furious nobody.

I grab the invitation, the tiny card, the envelope in my big paw hands and crash toward the kitchen. I kick over the kitchen table, the old kitchen table at which I was tortured meal after meal. It hits the floor with a satisfying thud. The ashtray lands with a clatter and the books spill into a lumpy pile. I leap out the front door. The screen *flap flap flaps* as I run with that invitation between my teeth, deeper and deeper into the woods toward Vick Street and home.

First I try to dig a hole in the ground and bury the stolen invitation. Then I think I should burn it, but the thing about me and fire is that I do not want to burn the invitation, I want to burn myself.

I think about it for a long time. I bring the invitation up to my room, set it on my music stand, and pick my violin out of its case. The invitation suddenly is music. I put my violin to my chin and read the invitation, it makes a tune, soft, sweet, tremendously sad. It carries me far back to a place even *Zaideh* Yitzhach won't remember. A place where even he might be safe from exile. I draw my bow from string to sorrowful string. In my head, women dance slowly, sadly, at first, then pinch each other's cheeks, stomp heartily into one another's arms. I, Nadine Pagan, play amidst these women. Dressed in flowing robes the women encircle me, gather me up, carry me swaying. I play my strongest, my loveliest, just like Minnie taught me.

Then a terrible thing happens. The women change into members of our family. Our mother carries me now, like a bundle of flaming rags, to a trash can. Daddy fans the flames. You, Jane, sprinkle me with a watering can. My music becomes frantic and terrible. It is all I can do not to smash the violin to bits.

I put it down and pick up the card that you are supposed to fill out, only this time I do. With a red crayon I write this : *M* NADINE PAGAN (your daughter) MIGHT VERY WELL *will*_____ *will not*_____ *attend.* Then I draw an arrow, turn the card over, scribble this poem :

> *I still recall*
> *that fateful day*
> *I came*
> *I saw*
> *I went away. Maybe I'll see you.*
>
> *Your daughter,*
NP

I stick it into the tiny envelope. I bring it to the mailbox on the corner near my house. Good-bye down the river I sing as I push the message through the slot. Drift away to my family like a note in a bottle. Your shipwrecked daughter has found land at last.

Chapter 7

Répondez Si'l Vous Plaît

Just for the record, I am not the ogress of this story. I am not the monstrosity you and Jane would have everyone believe. Jane was very quick to tell what a terrible bully I was about my grandfather's violin and how I drove you to set your head on fire because of it, but that's her side of the story. I am painted as the evil queen mother here. Very ironic since I pushed all three of you "women" through my hips and into the world, I carried all three of you for nine months apiece. I fed you, clothed you, and do I hear one word of thanks? No, only accusations.

None of you girls lived without a roof over your head, you had every material comfort. Who paid the bills around here? Answer me that. Who bailed each and every one of you out of your messes? Your father and me. So you go insane one night and try to burn us all to dust and ashes, who gets blamed? I'll tell you who. Me. Did I ask you to drag my grandmother's candlesticks off the kitchen table and make like the towering inferno? Jane would like to think so, but Jane is wrong.

Nadine Morningstar—wait what do you call yourself now? Nadine P-A-G-A-N (*gotteniu*)—how would you feel if the shoe were on the other foot? If you were your own daughter? Say a prayer of thanks first thing in the morning that you are not. You or your turncoat sister Jane. For my money she's been in on this since the beginning. The two of you are thick as thieves, that's how I figure it. Otherwise how the hell did you get hold of that invitation? It was a set-up job from the beginning, if you ask me. *Get Mom*, that's what I call it. Jane never wanted to be part of the wedding in the first place. What better plan than to get you, her crazy sister Nadine, to wreck it? Burn it down right before my eyes just like you did your head. I should have let you fry.

It cracks me up, it really does. Here is Jane, thrilling at every juicy morsel that shows how I, the mother, inflicted horrible mental cruelty on my poor, helpless teenage daughter—you— how I ran around like a chicken with my head cut off and abused you. Well, let me point out that this is the same Jane who read *Portnoy's Complaint* in my living room and wanted to string Philip Roth up by his balls because he had no respect for a Jewish mother. Do my daughters have respect for me? Answer me that!

You know, it wasn't any picnic raising three children in the '50s and '60s—three girls at that—and one of them, may God strike me mute if I'm lying, stark raving out of her mind. It was no picnic, but I don't see anyone handing out Gloria Steinem points for that.

Look at things for two minutes from my point of view if you'd be so kind. Imagine that one of your daughters—the one you had the stormiest days and nights with, the one who set her head on fire and then left you to sift through the ashes looking for a clue—imagine this daughter can't stand living with you, she hates you, so she goes and lives with your own mother. If you could stop thinking only about yourself for a minute and listen, you would remember that things were not always so hotsy-totsy between my mother and myself. My mother, the same expert who always said you would win prizes with that *geshtrofteh* violin, treated me, you will recall, like a talentless nobody. Your sister Jane says as a musician I had no enthusiasm. There she is partially correct. On the piano I had no enthusiasm. What did I have instead? Disappointment, and plenty of it. I have had a bitter taste in my mouth for fifty years.

Alright, Nadine, so not only do you go live with my mother who, despite her feelings about me and my abilities treats you like a queen, what do you do to show your thanks? You run away! I don't need to tell you how that made me feel. I was furious. I was humiliated. I could have killed you. But what good would that do? I killed myself instead. Not in reality, obviously. Here I am to tell about it now. But believe me, in a figurative way, I died. I was half dead. I know without listening to Jane, she doesn't have to tell me. A woman doesn't spend three-quarters of her daily life lying on the couch staring at the TV set, and the other quarter making dinner, without getting the message that something is wrong. It was like a big magnet was holding me to the couch day in and day out, but who noticed? I wanted to move after a while but I couldn't. I'm lying. Somehow, every day, I got up just long enough to cook dinner. Your father ate it, but he never said anything about it—was it good, was it bad, he never said. He just read the paper and chewed, and I stared at the food on my own plate and pushed it around and then I cleared the table and washed the dishes and after that it was back to the couch.

Sometimes your father came into the living room and changed the channel and we watched TV together, but usually I fell asleep. He noticed me then, I know, because he woke me up all the time. "Fay," he said, "you're snoring." Then I dragged myself into the bedroom. The next thing I knew it was morning.

It was like someone put a giant anvil on my chest and then sat on it. To clean the house, tocook, I had to shove the anvil over, but then when I was standing, it was on my shoulders, my head. First the constant pressure weighing down down down. What did I do? What did I do to make my own daughter run away from home? And then the horrible nagging from everyone around me—your Aunt Miriam, Grandma Minnie—where's Nadine? No word from her, Fay? All very well-intentioned mind you. Miriam even offered to pay for a private detective. Your father and I considered it, but in the long run what was the point? You were eighteen years old, this was the mid-1970s, a child was not one's own, you couldn't make them live at home until they got married like they did to us in the old days. You did what you wanted to do and that was the end of that.

Believe me, it was all I could do to keep myself from jumping in front of a bus. Thank God I didn't have the energy. One thing I'll say, we never gave you up for dead. Another family might have sat *shivah* for someone like you, but not us. *Eppes*, another family would have sat *shivah* for Jane, we never did. You think it didn't hurt us when we figured out Jane was a lesbian? Killed us! She says we never noticed her overalls. We noticed them. I saw how short her hair had become, but we were so happy she came home once in a while for dinner, we never said one word. Not one word, including *shivah*. Maybe we never had a lot of enthusiasm, but we were always glad to see her.

I always knew you were alive, Nadine. I thought you might be hiding in our basement, that's how strongly I felt you. I started counting the canned goods down there, kept an eye on the liquor, but nothing changed. Everything was as it always was, nothing was missing. Only you.

If you were dead my grandfather, may he rest in peace, would have come into my dreams to tell me. Correction. To blame me. In fact, I thanked God every day since you mailed that vandalized R.S.V.P. back that you were not dead because if you were dead and I think things are bad for me now, multiply that *tsores* by a thousand and that's a pretty good idea of what the blame quotient would be. Every ounce of blame would be on me. Your father never said it out loud, he never says it, but I know he blamed me when you ran away in the first place. He never really blamed me about the hair, but boy oh boy, after you took off from my mother's it was written all over him like with magic marker: YOU DID THIS, FAY.

Unfair, I say, unfair. Your father blames me because you ran away just like Jane blames me because you set your head on fire. But I'm here to tell you: I may have picked on you, I may have been sharper with you than seemed right, but I never ever drove you out of this house. Flesh and blood, as gory as it gets, is always welcome in this house.

When Electa announced she was getting married, I became a changed person. Thank God for that Mickey, God bless him, that boy saved my life. I swear to God, if he hadn't proposed I'd be lying on that couch watching soap operas this very minute. Worse yet, I would have figured out how to throw myself under a bus. Instead I threw myself into Electa's wedding.

I checked with every caterer in New England—Boston, New Hampshire, Vermont—everywhere. Still, the best price was one right here in Worcester. They came very highly recommended and offered everything: old-time Jewish food like *kishkeh* and *k'nishes*, as well as the more modern stuff-little hot dogs, chicken wings, things of that nature. Our menu was planned out perfectly. We were going to have the works, from soup to nuts. Fabulous "horse's doovers" followed by golden matzoh ball soup, and then you had a choice for the main dish between chicken or fish—everything kosher of course. I had eaten this particular caterer's food before at Alan Hirshfield's *bar mitzvah*, so I knew it was going to be delish, absolutely first-rate. And I knew just which printer to call for the invitations and exactly where to take Jane and Electa for their gowns. If you would have been here I would have gotten you a gown too. You might have looked lovely.

It was as if all of a sudden I woke up one morning and my reason for living was made crystal clear. My eldest daughter's wedding, what better reason to come back to the land of the living. It was as complicated as making a movie. I had to get the synagogue, rent the hall for the reception, I had to figure out the flowers for the *chuppa*, organize the centerpieces for the table, book the rabbi, send out the invitations, wait for the returns, plan the seating arrangements—it takes hours, weeks, months to plan a wedding. I was happy for the first time in years.

You entered my mind, Nadine, you came to my dreams, just so you know. A day did not go by when I did not have some thought of you, some pain in my heart. But planning Electa's wedding was like a trip to the curative spas. I had so much to do I couldn't possibly dwell on you or torture myself with memories of your hair sprouting fire in every direction, your sullen stares into the ground, your vile lips smirking at the back of my head. I was alive again. My mind full of details, I was as happy as possible for a woman in the 1970s with one lesbian daughter and one lunatic daughter who was missing in action.

I only wish I had listened to Electa and hired someone to open the returns. When she was around, we did it together. But she was in Boston visiting Mickey's parents, and I sat at the table defenseless. I opened that envelope from you, Nadine, and you might as well have stabbed me through the heart with a knife.

It looked like every other return when it came in the mail. How was I to know when I opened it what a letter bomb it contained. I should have held it under water. Instead, I brought it to the table. I had the routine down pretty good. First I opened all the envelopes with the letter opener Mel bought me special so I wouldn't ruin my nails. Then I pulled all the returns out and stacked them in a neat pile. I got out the guest list and a pen and marked the guest name appropriately with a *Y* or an *N*, and then the number of guests in their party. All of them were pretty standard fare, just the *will* or *will not* checked off, but one of them jumped out and grabbed me by the throat. No *will* or *will not* for this one. Instead it read : *M* NADINE PAGAN (your daughter) MIGHT VERY WELL *will*_____ *will not*_____ *attend*. Then on the back, in what looked like red lipstick or crayon, or possibly blood, it said:

> *I still recall*
> *that fateful day*
> *I came*
> *I saw*
> *I went away. Maybe I'll see you,*
>
> > *Your daughter,*
> > *NP*

As you might well imagine, I couldn't believe my eyes. I turned that R.S.V.P. card over and over in my hand in search of some other clue that would help me figure out exactly what that *vildeh chei-eh* brain of yours was trying to tell me. Were you coming to the wedding or not? How did you get hold of the invitation to begin with? The postmark said New Chelm. Jane lived near New Chelm. Did she find you and convince you to do this? How could she have found you and not bothered to tell us? It was treason on Jane's part. Treachery!

The poem on the back, what I could read of it, sent chills down my spine. Was it a direct reference to *Zaideh* Yitzhach's violin? Or the night you lifted my grandmother's candlesticks to your *tsedraiter* head? Of course it was! You were punishing me, Nadine. You hadn't shown up around here for God knew how long and this is how you would come back home. No mistake about it, the message was hostile, written in red for all the world to see: Nadine Pagan might possibly attend and a bizarre message on the back. No greeting. No indication that we had not seen hide nor hair of you, that you hadn't even had the decency to pick up a telephone and call any of us for over five years. Except, of course, Jane. Most definitely Jane.

I tapped the edge of the white card against my teeth. I felt a little nauseous and a little numb. I busied myself with my mother-of-the-bride-to-be chores but felt no joy. I watered plants, folded laundry, went shopping at the supermarket, but none of that erased the red writing, the strange poem on your R.S.V.P. I felt my old heaviness drift over me, the anvil on my shoulders and chest, that ponderous urge to lie down in the street and wait there for the bus.

Finally it was time to make dinner. Like a robot I prepared a lovely London broil, green beans and almonds, baked potatoes. I sat down at the kitchen table to wait for your father. At each passing car, I pricked up my ears like some dog, then folded my hands and waited some more.

I thought, and tapped, and bit at the card. Hadn't I already paid and paid? My own daughter! Why do you torture me?

Then I wondered. What harm would it be if you did show up as a member of the wedding? Would it be so horrible? Couldn't we cover up your ugly scar with pancake and creams? If we acted right away, wasn't there time for plastic surgery? We offered

67

before, we could still do it now! Maybe your voice didn't sound so bad anymore—you wouldn't have to open your mouth even, you could nod and smile politely standing there in the receiving line. As I saw it, the big problem was going to be getting you into a dress. Sure, you could come, I just didn't want you showing up in a pair of ripped jeans or a flannel shirt.

What was I talking about! What was I saying? You had just mailed us a reply to an invitation we never even sent. You were threatening to come to Electa's wedding and we had no way of knowing when or where you would appear. You were capable of any kind of diabolical magic. There was no way to control you. Was that what this little white card meant?

I heard a car door slam and jumped to the window. It was your father. I tried to go to the door to greet him. My feet were made of lead.

When your father was at last eating his dinner, I sat across from him and tossed him the ruined return. It narrowly missed the puddle of catsup that bordered his steak.

"What does it mean?" I asked.

He lifted the card close to his face. He immediately recognized your wild handwriting. "What does it mean? It means maybe she's coming and maybe she's not. How did she get hold of this anyway?"

I shrugged my shoulders. "Maybe Jane."

"You think Jane did this?" your father asked, pointing a forkful of steak at me. "What a wedding present for Electa." Mel's sarcasm was thick. As far as you were concerned, his heart was stone. And now here was your first message, frosting on the cake. After all we had done for you, shit was what we got.

Your father stuck a chunk of pink meat into his catsup. "You know what this is, Fay? This is spite. Pure and simple."

"But where's the joy in it?"

"That's the beauty of spite, Fay. It's its own reward."

I paced back and forth between the kitchen table and the dishwasher. Your father continued to cut and chew.

"I'm calling Jane." I said finally.

"Leave Jane out of this."

"Leave her out of this? As far as we know she's the cause of it. They're two of a kind. The only difference is, Jane used to know which side her bread was buttered on."

Your father dabbed his mouth with the edge of his napkin and smacked his lips. "If our beloved Nadine decides to show her face after all this time, let her. I'll give her the back of my hand but good, which is something I should have done years ago." He picked his teeth with the corner of a matchbook. "We have enough heartache now, Fay. The one we'll get if Nadine appears at this wedding will be bigger by far, believe you me."

"But suppose Nadine doesn't come to the wedding and convinces Jane to do the same?"

"Then it's good riddance to bad rubbish."

The kitchen was quiet as we stared off into our separate space. "Did you get enough to eat, Mel?" I asked as I pulled myself up to clear his plate.

"Believe me, Fay, I couldn't touch another thing."

Chapter 8

Up Against The Wall, *Mameh*

Two weeks before the wedding I was called to Worcester for an emergency meeting. My mother told me it was because my shoes didn't come out the right color. I was getting really sick of being at their beck and call every minute for this wedding, especially for a pair of stupid shoes. I had my own problems. The night I got back from my post-gown disaster dinner with Kria I came home and found my apartment an absolute wreck. Someone had broken in and trashed the place. They didn't even bother to take anything, they just messed it up—kicked the table over, threw my books around, broke an ashtray. It was totally senseless, and I was very jumpy. I didn't know what it meant and I absolutely didn't feel safe. In fact, one way I was going to try to get myself to feel safer was to go to the Take Back the Night march with Kria and my other friends so I could stop feeling scared.

It came out rude. "Look," I told my mother, "you know what size I wear, get the exact same pair and have them done over. What's the big deal?"

"Oh, fine, that's just fine," my mother's voice was dripping with sarcasm. "What did I expect?" she spat, then slammed the phone down in my ear. I paced around my kitchen and was about to call her back and apologize when the phone rang again. I picked it up gingerly.

"Jane, this is Electa. It's extremely important that you come in for dinner tonight."

"Jesus Christ, Electa, I know your wedding is the most important thing in the world to you right now but I have other stuff to do—tonight is Take Back the Night for chrissakes! If Ma is so worried about the shade of those shoes, she can deal with getting me another pair—"

"The shoes didn't come out exactly right, but that was just an excuse. We have a much bigger problem."

"I have a big problem too, Electa. I'm marching in Take Back the Night, there's a march up and down Main Street, it's a big community event—" and, I neglected to say, the woman I love wouldn't believe that I'm ditching out of it because my shoes of the patriarchy were the wrong shade of pink.

"How many times am I going to get married, Jane?"

"Don't do this to me, Electa—" I could feel my will begin to slip away, "Why can't Mommy just deal with the shoes?"

"It's not the shoes, Jane. This is an emergency—"

"What is it?"

"Come home and we'll talk about it."

I was really angry but I couldn't tell Electa that. She was getting married in two weeks. I couldn't tell my mother how mad she made me. She might blow up and spend the whole wedding pouting. I couldn't say anything to Kria either. She'd just tell me to get over it. I sat down on the floor under the kitchen table and lit a cigarette. "Can you give me a hint?"

"Mommy said to tell you dinner's at six."

I looked at the clock over the stove. "My God, Electa, it's almost four-thirty."

"If you leave now you'll make it. We'll wait."

Before I even got out of the car my mother was waiting for me at the front door. She was fanning herself with a small piece of paper. She threw the screen door open. "Don't you have a bag?"

"I'm not spending the night—"

I tried to hug her but her arms were folded now across her chest.

She was nodding her head frantically. "Don't do me any favors."

She hadn't moved from the doorway, so I still wasn't in the house. Electa poked her head over my mother's shoulder. "Hi, baby, thanks for coming! Ma, move over and let Janie in—"

"She's not spending the night," my mother said tersely.

"OK, but what's she gonna do, eat dinner on the porch?"

By now my father was hovering in the background, and I could barely see the top of Mickey's head over my mother's other shoulder. "Ma, I have to pee. Will you let me in so I can use the bathroom?"

She stormed away from the door. My father stood shaking his head. I tried to hug him but he was following my mother into the kitchen. I could hear her muttering under her breath.

"Hi, kiddo," Mickey said. He winked at me.

"What is going on here?" I whispered.

"Big crisis." He looked so serious I thought for sure my grandmother had contracted some fatal disease.

"Bubby?"

"Worse," he said.

I tiptoed into the bathroom and sat there for a few minutes trying not to think. I held my breath. What could be worse? Was my father sick? My mother? Had Electa come down with peritonitis now, just weeks before her own wedding? I washed my hands and went into the kitchen. The table was full of food, and my mother was fussing over something in the oven. I could hear Mickey and Electa's hushed voices in the living room.

"So what's up?"

My mother spun around and held that little piece of paper in front of my face. "How did Nadine get hold of this?" Suddenly she had me pinned against the kitchen counter. I was afraid she was going to choke me. I wanted to scream for help, but I was in my mother's own kitchen and who would help me there?

"I don't know what you're talking about," I gasped.

"I'm talking about this!" she pushed the little paper closer so I could see it. It was an R.S.V.P. card with red writing all over it. It looked like blood.

"How would I know, Ma?"

"It's postmarked New Chelm. That's where you live isn't it? Didn't you give this to her?"

There was a long kitchen knife on the counter beside us. I was finally terrified enough to yell. "Electa!" It came out weak and half-baked.

"What does Electa have to do with this? Why didn't you tell us you found Nadine?" She had her hand up and I could tell she was ready to slap me when Electa and Mickey both appeared behind her.

"Ma, what are you doing? What are you doing there, Ma? Get off her!

As suddenly as she had me pinned, my mother tossed the card at me and walked away. Then she spun around again. Electa put herself between us. "You found her, you gave her that invitation, you encouraged her to wreck this wedding!"

"You should have told us you found her, Jane," Mickey said in a rather officious voice, although you could tell he was trying to sound casual.

"What is everyone talking about?"

My mother tapped her foot. God knows where my father was hiding. I could hardly breathe.

"Read the card, Jane," Electa said. I read the front, then turned it over. "*I still recall that fateful day*—" I said out loud.

"Stop, I don't want to hear that one more time!" my mother opened the oven, looked inside, shut it off, then slammed the door. "My *kugel* is totally dried out."

"You're gonna blame me for that, too? I don't know how Nadine got a hold of this. Ma, I didn't give it to her, honest—"

Electa and Mickey had backed off and were sitting at the kitchen table. Electa poured herself a glass of Manischewitz and knocked the whole thing back in one swallow. Mickey ran his fingers through his hair and started pacing like my father who all of a sudden was standing right beside my mother. "You admit you know where she is," he snarled. "New Chelm is the size of a postage stamp, you had to run into her."

I sat down heavily next to Electa. "I don't know where she got that invitation, Daddy, I never gave it to her, I swear."

All at once it came clear. That stupid break-in, the papers spread everywhere, the table overturned. Everyone was looking at me like I just burned the house down. I took my keys out of my pocket and walked shakily toward the door. My mother thrust her arm out and blocked my path. My father and Mickey looked the other way. "The rehearsal dinner is the thirteenth at six o'clock. Come dressed in something decent."

I nodded my head and pushed past her.

"At least have some dinner," Electa mumbled from the kitchen table.

"No, really, I'm not hungry," I muttered. If I took all the short cuts I might make it back to New Chelm in time to watch the marchers return.

Chapter 9
M.I.A.

Nadine, you were gone. Not your body, it was there alright, washing dishes, staring into space. But the rest of you was checked out, evaporated, dangerous to be around. Especially as a food chopper. Particularly for someone like me who might want to kiss you, etc.

You were skinnier than ever but you looked like you were carrying a million pounds on your back. When I talked to you you growled. It was almost like since that bizarro sister of yours made the scene the month before you got bigger and smaller at the same time. A real weirdness began to fill you, and no one could console you, not even me, Rose, your friend and sex pal right from the beginning.

You became furtive, Nadine, and frenetic simultaneously. We heard music from your Vick Street room, but in the middle it would stop. Sometimes there was silence behind the door, but other times there was crashing or scuffling or even sobs and screams. We began to wonder, all of us dykes in the Vick Street house, if you were even in there alone. It scared me very deeply to think that you might keep me out of your room but invite another woman in. It was important to me that only I was your truest friend. But no one ever saw anyone else go in your room, and no one ever saw anyone else come out, so I decided you were battling your own devils, making war on yourself. My status as most-needed friend was safe. Some of the women in the rooming house were terrified of what was going on in there, but me, I was only sad. I took to consoling myself with trips to Willa Kaufman's land out in the country where I had secretly started my own marijuana patch.

Willa Kaufman was generous with her money and land. She was an elder in our community (I think in her forties back then), and the wealthiest woman in New Chelm. Her land in the country was open to all. I went there by myself often to plant pot (which she did not know about) and to play in the woods. Many women knew about the land, but few women used it because it was far from New Chelm, nearly an hour, and most of those women were city dykes who had little time for the pleasures of baking naked in the sun.

One day I got this idea in my head that what you really needed to make you forget all about your sister and stop throwing your music stand around was a trip with me up into the country. I would provide a personally guided tour of my marijuana plants (complete with a sampling of the various buds and shake) and then up into the cliffs we would go to Willa Kaufman's famous hunting cabin. It was never used for hunting. Just a one-room shack really, but with a bed and a blanket and a lovely view of the valley below. I would take you there, Nadine, and together we would relax with sweet green smoke as our guide and so delighted would you be, so soothed and relaxed would you become, that you would forget all of your troubles, fall into my arms, and love me again like you did in the old days, because I was good to you and cared about your heart. Just thinking about it I was getting hot. Oh, I could hardly wait.

As fate would have it, the very next day was one of those spec-taculoso August mornings, no clouds, everything green and breathing. I knocked on your door all jolly and delighted. No one answered. I knocked again. Nothing. I tried the handle. The door was locked. Oh well, I thought, she's down at the restaurant already. I'll ask her there.

I smoked a joint on the way down the hill to work, mentally preparing myself for your yes answer, ready to cook hours worth of lesbular breakfasts until the restaurant closed and we could split for the country. Crystal was already there chopping and brewing, the potatoes were all ready for me to start frying and spicing, but someone was missing. You.

"Where's Nadine?" I asked.

Crystal shook her head. "Beats me," she said. "Nadine called me last night and asked me to work for her. I wasn't going to, but I need the money."

I was very freaked out and wanted to gather myself up and run back to Vick Street to find you, Nadine, find out where you were and tell you my plan. But I'd knocked on your door just a half hour ago and you hadn't answered, and besides, how could I leave Crystal alone to prepare the food, cook the breakfasts, and then wash the dishes? It wasn't sisterly. So like the good dyke I basically was at heart I pulled myself into the kitchen, laid out my cast-iron frying pans, and started the onions sizzling. But all the time I was flipping and frying I was also wondering, where is Nadine? Why is she missing? Who is she with? With each egg I cracked open I wondered if you were alone in your room, desolate, or had some strange woman, not me, taken you to a romantic hideaway as I was planning to do? Was this stranger soothing you right now, even as I was raging and slaving over a hot stove doing my civic duty as a feeder of lesbians on a beautiful summer day?

Several hours later, having fed approximately fifty dykes five variations of hash-browned potatoes, eggs fried, scrambled, and baked in every possible cheese and vegetable combination known to woman, and not a few stacks of whole wheat, whole grain flapjacks smothered in butter and maple syrup, after scraping the crud off of all of their dishes and shoving them unceremoniously into the electric dishwasher, then putting them all away, I fished another joint out of my pocket and smoked it all the way up the hill to 66 Vick Street in search of you, Nadine Pagan.

Even though I lived there myself I crept up the stairs and tip-toed down the hall to your room. Carefully I laid my ear to the door. Someone was in there alright, most likely you, but were you all by yourself or was there another lover in there with you? The fact was, I could hear a lot of rustling behind that door. What could that mean? I rapped gently. The rustling stopped, but no one answered. I waited. The rustling started again, I knocked one more time and whispered (don't ask me why, it was two in the afternoon), "Nadine, it's me, Rose. Can I come in?" There was silence again, then the door opened a crack, then nothing, so I pushed it and found you alone (I sighed) sitting cross-legged on the floor with an array of maps in front of you. You didn't look up. Instead you put the maps behind you and stood up.

"Planning a trip?"

You shrugged and kicked back at the maps a little so I wouldn't look at them even by accident. I felt suddenly incredibly strange. I was a fool. I didn't belong here in my best friend's/lover's room. Worse yet, you weren't even my lover anymore. I wanted to go down the hall to my room and get some more pot but I was sure you would be gone if I left you alone even for a minute. "I was thinking," I said as casually as I could, "about taking a little trip myself. Just for the day. Up to Willa Kaufman's land. I thought we could hike around. It's not all pleasure you know, I have to do a little work in my garden, but still, it will be fun. What do you think, Nadine? It's really special up there, and I'd love to take you."

You looked at me and scratched your head. Your hair hung loose and crazy. You reached behind yourself for a Massachusetts map and shoved it in front of my face. You had traced some roads over with a red crayon. "Show me where."

"How come you have all these maps anyway?"

You acted like you didn't hear me, so I acted like I never said it and looked for Leveret and Shutesbury. "Here it is, right up here near Route 2." You pulled your fingers through your hair, then traced another line with a bony finger. You looked up quickly and said, "How long till we go?"

I couldn't believe you wanted to do it. "I'm ready any time." I said. Really I wanted to take a shower and change my clothes, but I was afraid if we didn't get into my car right that minute, you would change your mind.

"I will be ready in forty-five minutes," you told me, very serious.

I ran down the hall to get changed.

You met me on the sidewalk in front of the rooming house with a knapsack and a jacket and even your violin. "You *are* planning a trip. This place is only an hour away." Secretly I hoped you had a mushy idea to play me some pastoral love songs out in the country and had brought all that stuff with you so that we could be sweethearts together in the wilderness. You would open to me, and I would soothe you, and the two of us together would be healed.

You blinked and curled your fingers around the handle of your violin case. "OK," I said, "let's go."

Sometimes I could loosen you up and get something like a conversation going, or at least you'd laugh at my jokes or tell me sort of one of your own, or at least stare out the window and look excited. But today, no such luck. It didn't matter that the sky looked like it just walked off a postcard or that the air was totally clear for the first time in a month. It didn't matter to you at all. You just stared straight ahead and wouldn't answer me no matter what I asked you or what I said.

Finally, I decided to get into my driving and forget about trying to cheer you up or getting you to like me again. I gave up all hopes for a private concert in the woods. I flew over the curves all the way up to Willa's land like a pro, which is no mean feat in a VW. Then I down-shifted and eased the car up a bumpy dirt road and into the open field where I always parked. I made up my mind to ignore what a bummer you were being and enjoy myself. It wasn't so easy. How could I act like I didn't even care about you, Nadine? Even though Willa Kaufman's land is my favorite place in the world, and I did love the birch and pine woods and the stony cliffs. For me this was much more home than that tiny room up in Vick Street. The only reason I lived *there* was to stay close to you, and that was beginning to seem stupid. It was depressing living right down the hall from you and never seeing you, just hearing you go crazy. Boy, I was getting madder and madder as I walked over stones, past little streams, into the woods.

You were right behind me, but you might have been a million miles away. We hiked up into a clearing past the river that cuts through the land. Maybe I'd work on getting my own apartment. Maybe I didn't need to live with all those other dykes. Maybe I didn't need to live so close to you, stupid Nadine. Then you'd like me again because you know what they say, absence makes the heart grow fonder. We were about a minute away from my pot plants. I had to talk to you. "You got to promise me you won't tell anyone what I'm about to show you," I said, all the time thinking, *Big deal, you don't talk to anyone anyway. What're you going to say?*

We scrambled up a rock ledge to another clearing, and I spread open my arms wide. At first you didn't know what I was showing you. Then you saw 'em—tall, bushy, five-finger leaves, sweet and green. "Remember that pot I turned you on to the first day we met? I saved the seeds and here's what I got—my future in twenty-five hand-grown, all lesbian, sticky sweet sinsemilla plants." I squeezed a bud between my fingers and held it up for you to smell. To my surprise you sniffed it and smiled.

I am really a sucker. You smiled like that, and my heart turned into Velveeta cheese. "Nadine," I said, "where have you been?"

Your eyes narrowed. "Right here."

I sat very close to you. I wanted to put my arm around you but I wasn't sure I should. Our noses almost touched. "I can hear you in your room lately. It sounds like you're dying in there. I never know what I'm supposed to do." I did reach out and put my hand on your neck. "I miss you so much, Nady." Before I knew it, my mouth was this close to yours and we were kissing. "Oh, Nadine, I want you so bad." You held on to me, Nadine, and we kissed some more. At least five minutes I'd say. Then all of a sudden, you pushed me away and looked me right in the eye.

"Do not kiss me more."

"Why not? God, Nadine, it used to be so much fun with you. Come here—"

Then I did something really stupid. I mean something if a man did it I'd want to kill him. I fucking grabbed at you and tried to kiss you again. At which point you slapped me pretty hard on the mouth and bolted, I mean grabbed your knapsack and took off crashing through the woods.

"Hey," I called after you, "Nadine, hey, I really am sorry!" I kind of ran after you, but you weren't slowing down, and I already felt bad enough for acting like some boy with a hard-on so I just hollered out as loud as I could, "Meet me back at the car when you're ready to go home!" I knew that was stupid. I knew you were gone in more ways than just down the path and into the woods. I took a minute and then went about my business. I pulled weeds and pinched the buds back on the female plants, clipped the bigger leaves off the males. I made my way back up to the cliffs and looked in the cabin to see if maybe you were there. No such luck. I rolled a joint and sat out on the cliffs and smoked. It was over between us. Maybe not our friendship, but for sure we weren't lovers anymore. I closed my eyes. You wouldn't be down by the car waiting. I knew that. Somewhere inside me I knew something really bad had happened. I'm not saying my kissing you that way after you told me not to is the whole reason for everything that happened next. But when I finally made my way down to my yellow bug, saw not you nor even your violin, I knew you were gone from me for a long, long time.

Part 2

Chapter 10

Dancing In The Ark

Through the night I am running, my cheeks brushed by branches, my feet caught in brambles, my back on fire, my hair on fire, I run, twigs snap, I run, I lean against a mossy tree and pant like a dog until my breath becomes human and then I run again, not toward New Chelm but away from it, not away from our family but home.

Through the woods, over back roads I travel, I run, and when I can no longer run I walk, and when I can walk no longer I run again, on asphalt, in mud, through burdock and thorns, until the sun finally rises pink and scorching in the August sky.

Salty tears mingle with the sweat of my brow, I stumble but I never stop, I do not stop running until I see the dome of Temple *Beth Shalom* gleaming in the new sun, even then I do not stop but trip up onto the manicured synagogue lawn, dive into the bushes along the Western Wall, and there do I rest, face down in the bushes, more than rest, finally I sleep, nestled against the holiest wall of what is called God's house, my face cradled in my muddy hands, my violin a pillow for my weary head, the very first guest at our sister Electa's wedding, and uninvited at that.

On my belly in the bushes, flat like a worm, a snake in the grass, I sleep and dream. Never a bridesmaid, nor am I a bride, I dream of flames licking the walls of my attic room at Vick Street, of you, Jane, and our sister Electa, who run off hand in hand without me, of our mother and father, who find me, a corpse in the bushes, and chase me away from the wedding with knives.

I wake up to the sounds of wedding traffic: the florist who has come to decorate the *chuppa*, the baker who has come to decorate the cake, the hairdresser who has come to decorate our sister the bride.

I put my ear to a stained-glass window and from deep inside the temple, beyond the beveled glass, I hear our mother's voice. "Flowers," Fay is saying, and "pink," but someone is coming. I drop back down to the ground and hear no more. I want to sit all the way up and peek into the sanctuary, but here on my belly, I know my power. I have only to show the top of my wild head and all hell will break loose. For I am the daughter with the bloody fingers and the dirty mouth, the sister who burned a ring around my own face and lived.

I lie behind the bushes. The wedding guests arrive. Some I know from the sounds of their voices, others by the perfumes they wear. How tempted I am to join them. How well I know what bedlam that means.

So I lie, barely breathing, and watch the back door of the temple to make sure the coast is clear. I crawl on my belly to the open door, then leap through it like a wild cat. With my back to the wall I creep through corridors to the Hebrew school which smells, even after all these years, like poured concrete and linoleum, new textbooks and chalk. I duck into the girls' bathroom, ancient stomping ground, land of stolen cigarettes smoked with girls who detested me, even before I made the purple scar around my face. They tolerated me long enough to smoke cigarettes I stole from our father. Before I burned my head to bits and matches were money, not danger in my hands.

Here in the Hebrew school girls' room, I unzip my jeans and pee a day and a night's worth of pee, pour out my bladder and map my next move. Where can I watch this spectacle as it unfolds? How can I hide beneath the noses of so many who know me?

While all of the wedding guests in fancyschmanz dresses and rented tuxedos prepare to float into *shul*, I, Nadine Pagan, monster Morningstar, trained by stray cats in two towns to walk in the dark, creep along the hallways of Temple *Beth Shalom*, my violin tucked under my arm like a machine gun, and disappear. Where am I going, Jane? Where have I gone? Only keep looking. You'll find me soon.

Look closely. Does the light flicker oddly from within the Holy Ark? Is there a woman pressed in between the *Torah* scrolls? What is she doing? What does she want? Is she hugging those *Torah* scrolls or pissing on them? Is she devouring the *Torah* scrolls? Eating them word by holy word, phrase by contentious phrase? She could be a member of this wedding, march down the aisle in a once-in-a-lifetime dress, hold her own personal bridesmaid bouquet, if only she could find it within herself to cut her hair put a layer of pancake make-up around her purple scar agree to dance the hootchy-cootchy and do the twist if only if only if only. But I am Nadine Pagan, a tough cookie to crack, a rough nut to crumble. I will never settle for basic black and a simple strand of pearls, I'd only look like a broken-down velveteen chair, stuffing falling out of me. Not this Nadine Pagan. I remain hidden, never speak even when spoken to, joyless at the celebration of our own sister's wedded bliss. This Nadine Pagan has fallen overboard. This Nadine this Nadine this Nadine is nothing if not hidden watching from the wings, studying firsthand and up close the lush satin and velvet robes of the *Torahs*, the sparkling silver crowns and breastplates, how I wish the rabbi would open the Ark, take me out and cradle me in his rabbinical arms, walk with me among the congregants to be kissed and blessed blessed and kissed, how I wish someone would hold me up on the *bima*, untie me, unravel me, read my wisdom and stories out loud, bring blessings one to the other from inside of me, the holy teachings of Nadine, my own code of ethical love:

*inthebeginningwasthefire*haesh
whichburnedonherheadandthroughher
brainthendownintotheheartofherthe
cuntofherthetoesofher

Here are the words of Nadine Pagan, elegant monster. Translated, her wisdom means this:

DONOTSPEAKONLYBURN
DONOTBURNONLYVOMIT
DONOTVOMITONLYRUN
DONOTRUNONLYBURN
ONLYBURNONLYBURNONLYBURN

The silver finger of the *yad* points at me word for mumbled word. What's this, the music is changing now, the pipe organ is switching from the liturgical white noise which welcomes in the wedding guests with ushers on their arms it brightens up a bit it lightens up a bit, in my mind's eye I see her, Temple *Beth Shalom*'s resident organist, the exciting, the daring, the most remarkable and ancient Mrs. Kaminer who has played for weddings and *bar mitzvahs* for well over twenty-five years. I imagine Mrs. Kaminer looking exactly as she did when I was a girl, only whiter, in her navy-blue beaded dress, the one she has worn to play at weddings and *bar mitzvahs* since I began to come to temple.

I peer out the crack in the Ark door and what do I see? With one eye I watch the wedding ballet begin.

How beautiful they all look in their wedding finery, the aunts and uncles, the neighbors and cousins, the family friends I haven't seen for years. How they drift into the sanctuary in their fabulous best, these dignified invited guests, and if I weren't such an upstart, such an abomination, I could be among them.

A man in a maroon tuxedo carries in on his dignified arm the grandmother of the bride, our own *bubby*, Grandma Minnie, the same Grandma Minnie who gave me our great-grandpa's violin and left me to fiddle myself out of the family, bent over now, wizened, barely able to hobble, but hobble she does down the aisle to watch her *shaineh maidel* granddaughter tie the knot. Then an usher escorts our mother Fay, who smiles bravely and dabs the corners of her eyes. She looks radiant and proud, even though she keeps glancing over her shoulder. Looking for me are you Fay? Looking for me? For a second, when Fay looks up at the Holy Ark, I shrink back. She knows I am here. I'll bet she knows I'm here.

The ushers deposit the mother and the Grandma Minnie of the bride into the best seats in the house, front row center, then go back to get the bridesmaids. My whole life floats before me as Electa's old friends from high school come down the aisle in their pink dresses and dyed-to-match shoes.

Then the best man comes down the aisle balancing a familiar figure on his arm. I know this woman, but I cannot place her. Wait, I get it, the woman on the arm of the man with the shiniest hair is you, my sister Jane, wobbling a bit on unsteady heels, your hair puffed up on your head, your eyes painted with blue shadow. You look like an air-brushed version of your self. Here, hidden between the *Torahs*, I can't tell, is your strange smile beatification or twenty years of stress and family strain?

The groom and the handsome young rabbi come out from the *bima* wings as if on cue. They stand under the *chuppa*, so close to the Ark I can almost touch them. The actors are in place, the rabbi nods his head, and from up above, Mrs. Kaminer belts out a stunning rendition of "Here Comes The Bride," and here comes that bride alright, Electa Morningstar, attorney-at-law, daughter of Melvin Morningstar, shoe salesman, and Fay Feldspar Morningstar, most efficient housewife in the world, here they both come, in fact, the bride herself and her smiling father, she, his most devoted daughter, in a long white dress, holding a bunch of pale roses, he, in shoes so shining and a tuxedo so snappy that he almost looks as if he's marrying Electa himself.

Mrs. Kaminer stops playing. Electa and Mel are so close to me I can smell Electa's hairspray. The rabbi starts speaking, I hear every word: They are gathered here today to join this man and this woman in a holy bond eternal. Their love is like a ring, it has no beginning and no end. Does Michael Robbins take Electa Morningstar and vice versa in sickness and health, 'til death do they part? They do? The rabbi says some words in Hebrew. I look out at my mother, who looks over her shoulder, up at the ceiling, toward the side doors. I look across to you Jane, you have a finger to your eye. Are you crying Jane, or is that only sticky mascara, I wonder, because I feel like crying myself. Not a snuffle or a trickle, I want to bellow so loud that the Ark doors will fly open like a holy sneeze, my sorrow will bless you all like no rabbi's words.

I don't know why, though. Weddings don't matter much to me, especially not with this talk about forever. The thought of forever with the same person, Rose Shapiro for example, year after year, that makes me want to cry too, but for different reasons which I also don't understand.

To stop the great sigh that wells up inside me, I, Nadine Pagan, hold my breath. I hold it and hold it until Mickey Robbins, All-American Jewish Boy Next Door, good in sports and pretty to look at, steps on the glass. In the crunch and under cover of a wave of congregational *mazel tovs*, I let out a tiny whelp, and shudder against my fellow *Torahs*. The glass is smashed, the bride kisses her groom, and I cannot help it, tears are falling fast from far down inside me. How I wish it was me, stomping on that glass and holding Electa in my arms. But now it is good-bye down the river, sweet sister Electa, good-bye, good-bye from the wolf girl, Nadine. Tears fall in torrential rivulets through the welts of my purple scar. I can't stop sobbing. An ages-old sorrow implodes, I cave in on myself like a thousand tons of TNT facing the wrong direction. The pressure it causes blows me out of the Ark, almost into Electa and Mickey's stunned arms.

Chapter 11

Lesbian Wedding Guest From Outer Space

It was a circus. There I was, dressed up like a wobbly French pastry, my pink roses wilting, my feet burning, my ankles killing me, watching my oldest sister, a lawyer-to-be who graduated top—*top* in her class—signing her life away to some guy, when my other sister, who no one but me has seen for half a decade, acts like a jack-in-the-box and jumps out of the Ark—the Holy Ark for God's sake—and lands on the rabbi. My balance was off already, I wasn't used to being bound in girdles and bras, then stood at a thirty-degree angle in dyed-to-match shoes. I was really something, let me tell you, a third-year dyke stuffed into a pink chiffon gown, lacquered down and painted with hairspray and eye shadow, eye liner and lipstick, mascara that stuck in gooey heaps at the corners of my eyes. Even my zombie self, who arrived in my place and against my better judgment at the rehearsal dinner the night before, couldn't block out the absurdity—me, a lesbian activist working on a double major in women's studies and pre-med, the maid of honor at my oldest sister's wedding.

Try as she might, neither could my zombie self stop me from thinking about the way my mother had shoved me around and tried to strangle me because she thought for sure I invited Nadine to the wedding, which I hadn't done. The remaining two weeks before the wedding I lived in dread. Should I have told them about the break-in? Should I have confessed that yes, I did see Nadine, but only for a minute in a lesbian restaurant in the town of New Chelm? Would that have prevented my mother from trying to strangle me? It didn't matter, I thought, we were all safe now, the service was over, Electa and Mickey were officially hitched. Nadine was not coming and was not here.

Then, all in a flash, there was Nadine. Her hair was flying every which way, her jeans were covered with mud, her vest was ripped to shreds, she looked really bad, and there she was, leaping out of the Ark and running down the aisle. The rabbi was flabbergasted. My father and Mickey looked like identical twins, frozen in place with their mouths wide open. Electa took off like a shot down the aisle after Nadine. I have to admit she ran pretty fast for someone fettered by a wedding gown. My poor mother, I really felt sorry for her. It was her worst fear come true.

The guests stood in worried groupings but stayed in their pews. Two of the other bridesmaids started to giggle, and one, a woman Electa had known since junior high school, was crying. After a minute or two, Electa appeared at the back of the synagogue shaking her head. Her veil was disheveled and frankly, I thought she looked terrific. She strode purposefully down the aisle. My mother went up to her, looking toward the back door the whole time. They conferred. My mother muttered something, then Electa shot her a look and my mother backed away, scowling. My father by this time had his hands in his pockets and was moving in a slow circle around his corner of the altar. Electa climbed back under the *chuppa*, whispered something to Mickey, who whispered something to the rabbi, who gestured toward the heavens and took his place before the congregation.

I found it interesting but not surprising that no one said anything to either my father or me.

"The, uh, bride, Electa Morningstar-Robbins, has asked me to apologize for this rather unusual disturbance. She has asked that there be no receiving line, but that you all take a few minutes and then please join her and her family at the reception, which will proceed as planned in the main social hall."

"You'll regret it!" came my mother's voice from the sanctuary.

Electa spun and stared. My father shrugged. I saw Mickey's mother Sima lean across the aisle to my mother and put a hand on her shoulder. To my surprise, my mother didn't push her away.

"The groom will kiss the bride," the rabbi said, full of false cheeriness. He kept glancing behind him toward the Ark as if to make sure we would be subject to no further attack. Mickey ran a hand through his hair and embraced Electa, but I didn't see them kiss.

"*Mazel tov*," my mother said joylessly. A trickle of echoing *mazel tovs* followed. The guests applauded lightly as Mrs. Kaminer played a recessional, and Mickey and Electa walked down the aisle together. Neither one of them smiled.

In the bridal suite I thought I would suffocate. "Look," my father was saying, "Electa is right. We spent a fortune on food, on liquor, the band is here already, we got people all the way from California. What are we gonna do, send everybody home?"

"How do you know she isn't going to burst in on the middle of the party and ruin it?"

"Could she hurt us any more than she already has, Ma?" Electa had her feet up on the dressing table and was smoking a cigarette. She looked really butch, and I wondered why I'd never noticed it before. Maybe it was the kind of butch that needed a wedding dress to set it off.

Mickey was sitting between his parents with his head in his hands. Through the wall I could hear the band playing some sappy Connie Francis tune. I slid a cigarette out of Electa's pack and lit it.

My mother turned on me. "When did you start smoking?"

I pretended I didn't hear her and said nothing. My father said, "Who cares, Fay. There are 150 people out there who came all this way to watch our oldest daughter get married. Everything is paid for, we can't send it back. If Nadine dares—dares—to show that purple face of hers in that social hall, I will personally kill her. This is my oldest daughter's wedding. I've waited my whole life for this party, and the last time we talked about it, Fay, you did too. We have a moral responsibility to live through this *shandeh*. As father of this family I command you, go out, get *shikker*, and have a good time!"

I wobbled into the party guardedly, not sure that Nadine wouldn't come jumping out from behind the head table or under the bandstand. I was adrift in a sea of gowns and tuxedos until my Uncle Al pinched my butt and brought me back to reality. Instead of hauling off and slugging him the way I wanted to, Zombie Jane smiled through my teeth and walked away. I endured more pinches at the hands of aunts and neighbors who pulled my cheeks and told me how good I looked. Had I lost weight? Who did my hair? The Zombie Jane thanked them and pushed on through the crowd. None of the wedding guests mentioned Nadine's sacrilegious somersault, but you could tell they were dying to. I threaded my way though the cummerbunds and petticoats that swirled around the social hall as waitresses passed trays of *kishkeh* and *k'nishes*, and uncles belted down schnapps and hit each other on the back over dirty jokes. It was unbelievable. It was as if nothing catastrophic had happened at all.

The band was one of those corny wedding affairs. We were doomed, I could tell, to dance the cha-cha and the hully-gully all night. They were playing "*Bay Mir Bistu Sheyn*" as I teetered toward the bar, and a glass ball spun bubbles of light over the dance floor. I wondered if I'd fallen into a freaked-out "Lawrence Welk Show," and how my sister Electa could agree to this, Nadine or no Nadine, how she could allow this to happen in her name. When *I* got married, Aretha Franklin would play at my wedding, I could see it now—150 lesbians in their best flannel shirts, twirling each other in pagan circles, asking my mother to dance.

I took my assigned seat at the head table next to Mickey's cousin Ben. He immediately began to flirt with me under the guise of asking what all that commotion was about at the end of the ceremony. Little did he know that beneath my lacquered, zombie exterior there lay a rabid dyke, ready to snap his head off at any moment. I smiled at Ben with glinting teeth. "What commotion," I said coldly. "That was my insane sister Nadine. She escaped from the asylum and decided to give us all a little thrill by locking herself up in the Ark. You might check with Mickey, but I believe they wrote it into the ceremony."

Ben blinked and immediately started flirting with the brides-maid sitting on his other side. I heard them both say, "Weird."

Before dinner we had toasts and more toasts. I think my father kept adding them to get everybody (i.e., he and my mother) as drunk as possible so that they'd forget about Nadine. First we drank to Electa and Mickey. Then a toast to my parents who pro-duced such a sweet and smart bride. Then a toast to Mickey's parents, producers of such a smart and handsome son. Then they surprised me by drinking a toast to me, the smooth-faced sister of the bride, most likely to get married next. Well then, I thought, tipping back my fourth glass of champagne, won't they be surprised when I walk down the aisle with a woman on my arm. And Nadine will be my maid of honor.

The waitresses brought bowls of golden chicken soup, each with a perfect matzoh ball floating precisely in its center. I dipped my spoon and sipped, and with this flavor, timeless and familiar, a crazy crying began inside me. It was ancient crying, hopeless and logical. Tears that made my make-up run, tears that started slowly but flowed ceaselessly. I didn't know where they came from or how to make them stop. Even Jane the Zombie, who wanted me to smile, could not gain back control.

No one else seemed to notice. My mother and father waved cheerfully as they danced by, although you could see my mother had her hackles up and hadn't yet relaxed. Maybe my tears were invisible, but I felt them flowing down my cheeks, over my breasts. I was alone at this wedding, on an island, floating, eating, ready to scream. And the irony of it all was that somewhere, hiding in the woodwork, was Nadine, my sister, who lived on the same little island as me.

When dinner came, I pushed my chicken and carrots around the plate. Aunt Miriam asked me to dance. I was surprised, it was a slow song, but I let her hold me in her warm arms, let my fingers rest on her girdled behind, sunk my head down on her welcoming breasts. I started sobbing. Did Miriam notice? If she did, she said nothing. When the song was over, she kissed me on the head and spun away into the arms of waiting Uncle Al.

I wanted to fix my face, and the Zombie Jane agreed. Wasn't my make-up running? Couldn't everyone see my sorrow? I drifted away from the dancing up to the Hebrew school, to the bathroom where I had hidden my tears in years gone by so many times before. Upstairs in this bathroom, the wedding party vibrating full tilt beneath me, I leaned against the cool porcelain sinks and pushed my shoes off. The linoleum was smooth under my feet. I stared into the mirror and saw the ghost of a woman I knew well. A woman with a sprayed helmet of hair and raccoon markings around her eyes. A freaked-out, lesbian Barbie doll. I couldn't control it at all now. I sobbed, alone, in the bathroom, into the sink. Me, Jane, the alien sister, the Martian. If Nadine would show herself again, we would at least be two. I could dance with her the way I had with Miriam. Maybe unconsciously I had wanted her to break into my apartment and find that invitation. Maybe, subconsciously, I wanted Nadine to marry me. We could have a big party and dance all night. No one would be forced to wear make-up or hairspray, or even bras. Girdles and high heels would be absolutely forbidden. Clothes would be optional. All of us could run around the temple naked like the matriarchs in the oldest days. Kria could come. She'd have a new lover by then, and everything would be fine because it would be my wedding, my wedding to Nadine, and only women would dance, together, under the *chuppa*, in the aisles, under the stars.

I found myself in the mirror again. I wanted to wash all the makeup off, all the hairspray, all the grief. I wanted to dance forever in another woman's arms, but I was alone in the bathroom. I sat on the floor and finally stopped crying. I breathed heavily and my sore heart pounded.

I pulled myself up and sprinkled cold water on my face. I scraped off the paint around my eyes with a paper towel. I could see it now, real skin, my own face, me, Jane Morningstar, lesbian activist, upstart and sister. The Zombie Jane was gone for the rest of the evening, exactly where she belonged.

Back at the party there was joyous drunk dancing. Uncles stooped down into knee bends and kicked their feet while more uncles stood around them in a circle and clapped. Aunts spun each other around in one another's arms. There were clinking glasses and dancing babies. Everyone seemed happy.

My Grandma Minnie had some archaic cousin from Boston up against the bar and was waggling her fingers at him. My mother was dancing in her stocking feet and at last seemed to be feeling no pain. Time dragged on until finally the bride and groom were ready to escape to their honeymoon. Mickey threw Electa's garter into a crowd of bleary-eyed ushers. Electa closed her eyes and tossed her bouquet. I caught it by accident and tossed it like a hot potato into the hands of Aunt Miriam. She grabbed it in spite of herself and started to laugh.

Electa came over to me and gave me a big hug and kiss. "Thanks for everything, sweetie. You did a great job keeping it together. Now keep an eye out for Mom."

My God, what a curse. Electa and Mickey at last ran out of the synagogue followed by parents, grandparents, cousins, and friends. They drove off in their shiny new car with old shoes and tin cans rattling behind. I suddenly realized that I was expected to stay at my parents overnight. There was no way I could do it without losing my mind. I broke it to my mother after she finished dancing the *hora* with a circle of my aunts and great-aunts. She was tipsy and radiant.

"How can you go, Jane? We have a big family gathering tomorrow, post-wedding brunch—"

My father was drunk and waved me away. "Let her go, Fay. She's probably got a date with that no-goodnik sister of hers, let her go and give Nadine a report of the big drama. Tell her, Jane, we had a big success in spite of her spectacle."

"Dad . . . ." I started to argue but saw it was useless. They walked me out to the car. I reached my arms out and gave them each hugs. To my surprise, they hugged me back. Then they trudged inside to the fading party. "How could two sisters be so different and look so much alike," I heard my father say. Was he talking about me and Electa or me and Nadine?

I tucked my dress tight around me and slipped behind the wheel of my car. Before I flipped the key into the ignition and started the engine I unhooked my bra. I buckled my seat belt, reached down and released the emergency brake, then breathed a sigh of relief. Out of nowhere a rough, greasy hand covered my mouth.

"Don't scream, I won't hurt you," a familiar voice scratched. "It's me, Nadine. Take me back to New Chelm."

Chapter 12
Smoke Wakes Up Your Thighs

I was sitting in my own bathtub, smoking my own joint, touching my own clit, trying to have my own good time and finally forget about everything, when all of a sudden there was scratching on the window. My own window in my new second-floor apartment in the middle of the fucking night. What was I trying to forget about? Well, for one thing, the fact that (a), you, Nadine Pagan, disappeared, vanished, never came back to your stupid little alcove of a so-called room at Vick Street, neither did you show up for work at *Lechem V'Shalom* after that day I slapped a make on you up on Willa Kaufman's land. I knew it was all my fault because what the fuck else could it have been? I mean, I went back down to my car that day and your knapsack was gone, your violin was gone, all your stuff. That was three days ago. Then (b), these flannel shirts I lived with there in the Vick Street rooming house the very night of that same day (they have such great timing), all at once, all together, got incredibly uptight about the fact that I was selling pot out of my own private room and told me I had to move out. Sheesh. I never had anyone come up to buy drugs who wasn't a woman or probably wasn't a lesbian either, right, but all those crew-cuts became anal-retentive simultaneously and started raving about security and privacy and every other woo-woo lesbian thing. Finally what they told me was, quit selling marijuana (they even called it *mari-juan-a* with their little tweaky noses in the air, sounding like they all had English accents) or get out of the house because I was putting everyone in jeopardy. That was the exact word they used, *jeopardy*. So I had to find a new place to live. Fortunately, one of my most trusted and respectable rich lesbian customers needed someone immediately to sublet her apartment for a few months, so I just moved everything (including all my big bags full of shake, flowers, and seeds) over to her place the very next day. She was totally cool. She even said it was OK to pay her rent in pot. Fuck, I didn't have any furniture or anything, but she had a queen-sized water bed and one of those big squishy couches you could disappear into and no one would ever know where you went, plus a color TV and a great stereo with the world's largest record collection—women recording artists from every genre and era. It was perfect. I showed those other dykes. They wanted me to move, fine. Bang, like that, something much better came along. I had my own kitchen and bathroom for the first time since I came out. I could take baths whenever I wanted to, just hang out in there and smoke a joint and not care what a bunch of flat tops with no sense of humor thought about my habits or my business or anything.

The only reason it wasn't perfect was that I didn't have a girl-friend. Not just any girlfriend, either. You, Nadine, in particular. Boy, I really missed you, and boy did I feel like an asshole. Not only did I scare you out of my life, I scared you all the way out of town.

These were my sad thoughts as I enjoyed the relative pleasures of a smoky bath with three white candles and Janis Joplin begging me from the stereo to *c'mon c'mon c'mon take it just another little piece of my heart,* when out of nowhere, there was scratching on the window and I came to attention there in the bathtub because it was three o'clock on a Saturday night and I was a woman alone. I wrapped myself up in one of these cushy blue towels that are overflowing from the closets around here and tip-toed into the living room. I turned Janis off and listened again. Sure enough—scratching. More than scratching, someone was rattling the bedroom window. So there I was, totally naked and pretty freaked out because, like I said, this apartment is on the second floor and it sure sounded to me like someone was trying to break in. Then I grabbed this wine bottle that's stashed with about fifty others on the bookcase, held it up like a frigging rolling pin, put on my best butch voice, and said, "Who's there?" What I got back was more rattling, and this raggedy-ass gravel voice saying, "Rose, let me in."

Sure, Nadine. It was you. Who else would it be? I went up to the window and there you were, hanging like some monkey from the woodwork. "What the hell are you doing there?"

"My hands hurt, let me in!"

I kind of stood there and thought about it for a minute. I mean, I missed you. I really did miss you. But this was exactly the kind of thing that always got me in trouble with you. You'd come around all broken down and I'd open my heart to you. Ten minutes later you'd hand it back to me all caved in and trashed. Still, I couldn't leave you hanging there like a monkey. "Come around to the back door, will ya?"

You let go and disappeared, and for a minute I was sure you had killed yourself. There were about ten seconds I didn't even care. Then I threw on my bathrobe and ran down and opened the door and Nadine, you practically fell into the house. I didn't want to be, but I was really glad to see you, even though you smelled bad. I didn't bother to ask you how you knew I was here. When we got upstairs you just stood there in the kitchen and hardly moved a muscle.

"You want some food or something? I just got out of the bathtub—the water's still kind of clean. No offense, but I think you need one. Go ahead, get in the tub; I'll make you something to eat."

You nodded your head slowly and tiptoed toward the bathroom. I heated up some soup that was left over from the restaurant and brought it to you in the tub. That was all I was going to do, clean you up, feed you some soup, and maybe let you sleep out on the couch. But when I saw you, your hair soaking wet, stretched out all skinny and exhausted with your eyes closed, I wanted to scoop you up in my arms and hold you forever. I sat down on the floor beside the tub. "Hey, I cooked this myself. It's beet borsht à la lesbo." You opened your eyes and stared at me like you didn't know who I was. I scooped up a spoonful of soup and held it to your mouth. You sipped it like a baby, then took the whole bowl from me and bolted it down. When you were finished I reached for the empty bowl. You laid back and closed your eyes again. I wanted you bad. Maybe I could let you into my heart this time and you would stay. Maybe we could be girlfriends together in this cushy apartment and never have to leave.

"So," I said, in my most casual voice, "where ya been?" You opened one eye, looked right at me, took a deep breath, then submerged yourself totally into the bathtub's depths.

We slept together in the water bed. It was better than my wildest dreams. We didn't even smoke dope or anything, and I didn't even make the first move. Before I knew it, you were lying naked next to me, then you were kissing me, then your hands were all over me, and I couldn't believe it. I didn't want you to stop. I mean it was a secret dream—I'm in a water bed in some ritzy-pitzy lesbian apartment, Janis Joplin is on the stereo, there is a scratch at the window, I open it, suddenly my best girlfriend bursts in on top of me, and we make passionate love for hours. Only it wasn't exactly like that. It was actually kind of weird because anytime I tried to touch you, Nadine, you pulled away or held my hands back. It was this stone butch number I had no idea you had in you. It went against my grain in a way because I'm one of those women who likes to, at least if you don't do each other at the same time, have some give and take. But you were into giving it, Nadine, and probably it did me good to just lie around for an hour and take it.

But then, this is the really strange part, when we were done, you kind of just rolled over and pretended to be asleep. Not me, boy, I was totally agitated. I leaned over and tapped you on the arm. "Nadine," I said, "does this mean we're girlfriends again?" You turned and faced me. I wanted to hold you, but you tightened up as soon as I touched you.

"We are always girlfriends," you rasped, then you rolled across to the furthest side of the water bed and fell fast asleep. After another hour of drifting listlessly toward dreamland, me, I fell asleep, too.

The phone started ringing at nine in the morning. I put my pillow over my head and ignored it. It stopped, but then two minutes later it started ringing again and I was pissed. Who the fuck was calling me at nine in the morning? I was having such a bizarre dream, too: Me and you were in a little canoe and it was all peaceful, and then all of a sudden we're going over Niagara Falls. Actually, it wasn't as scary as it sounds because the good part was, just at the minute we were going over the falls, you were about to tumble into my arms. That's when the phone rang. I tried to dive down further into my dream and those freezing Niagara Falls, but the phone wouldn't stop so I jumped up and grabbed it.

"Rose, this is Crystal. From the restaurant. You were supposed to be here an hour ago—"

"No I'm not. I don't work again until Sunday—"

"It is Sunday." She hung up the phone before I could tell her I'd be there in fifteen minutes. I threw myself out of bed, jumped in and out of the shower, pulled my overalls on, tied my shoes, and wrote you a note. Then I sat down on the bed by the pile of rumpled blankets thinking I'd sneak in one quick kiss while you were half asleep and wouldn't notice. Real quiet and mouselike I pulled the sheet back from your pillow all set to give you the world's sweetest, most sensitive, early morning lesbian kiss. What I found there instead was no Nadine Pagan at all. You were gone. Nowhere. I pulled the blankets all the way off the bed. I even looked down between the bed and the frame.

Not a trace.

I sat on the couch in the living room and rolled a joint. I lit it and took the scenic route to the restaurant, down the hill and through the woods. If I paced myself, I could smoke the whole number up and forget about everything before I even got in the door.

Chapter 13

Chicken Soup *Mit Kreplach*

I, Fay Morningstar, mother of the bride, at one time aspired to become a rabbi. As with my dream to become a world renowned concert violinist, my hopes were dashed to bits by incredulity and skepticism. Just as my hands were all wrong for fiddle and bow, so was my female soul unfit to dispense the wisdom and beauty of God. Just as my desire to play the violin remained with me my whole life long, it was my life's next wildest wish to be a holy of holies, free of you children altogether, except to pronounce upon you benedictions, wishes of good faith, luck, and love in the world. I wondered every day of my childhood and well into my adult years why there were no Jewish nuns, no women pillars of the faith, no Jewish convent I could run away to as a very young girl. How I longed to study *Talmud* and *Torah*, pronounce justice, and learn to play the violin as well.

I felt my dream of piety strongly when the rabbi came onto the *bima* to marry Electa and Mickey. How I wished it could be me who would bless your older sister and her lawyer-to-be husband, me who would sanctify their union of ever-lasting wedded bliss. Instead, I sat trapped in a pew, front-row center, pinned between your grandmother Minnie and my *machutonestah*, Sima, while Mel, your father, stood bursting his buttons up on the altar, giving our daughter away.

It was some compensation that instead of doing the actual marrying, I planned the most exquisite wedding party on the face of the earth. I organized everything, and like the greatest rabbis, I solved every problem.

I determined who would mingle, who would become stupid, who would talk too much, who would be struck dumb, and sat each guest accordingly at dinner. I took great pains to calculate what each guest would eat: how many *latkes*, *k'nishes*, and *kishkehs* would be served piping hot by crisply dressed waiters; how many rounds of rye bread smeared with chopped liver and herring; how many kosher hot dogs half the size of a thumb. The guests would require eighty-nine chicken dinners and sixty-nine roast beefs based on what they checked off on their R.S.V.P.'s. It was I alone who decided whether to serve green beans almondine or candied yams (I opted for the green beans, yams seemed so *goyisheh*), rice or potatoes (I decided on rice), traditional *challah* or nouvelle cuisine rolls (we would have both).

It was I who engaged the wedding orchestra, a quintet known for their ability to hack out old Yiddish favorites along with the latest hits, ordered the liquor, and arranged for the beautiful flowers which would sit in the center of each round table in the synagogue social hall. It was I who decided to make the gladioli on the *chuppa* pink in order to accent the lovely bridesmaid gowns.

I planned that wedding and the fabulous party that would follow down to the final toothpick in lieu of actually sending my daughter off into the world on a spiritual raft of *l'chayims* and *baruch atahs*. Now, at last, my moment was here. In a few short minutes Mickey Robbins would step on the glass and break it, the congregation would explode into a gentle chorus of *mazel tovs*, and Electa would walk down the aisle a married woman. We would, all of us—Mel, me, Jane, and the Robbins—stand and receive our guests, pose for pictures, eat and drink and dance up a storm.

Why then did I smell disaster in the air? A Nadine-related disaster, like the foul odor of your burning hair and flesh. I hoped

I was wrong. For this was my life 's finest moment in twenty years, since Jane was born. The mouths around me were watering. The ceremony was almost over. Mickey 's foot was poised above the glass. You were nowhere to be seen, your spoiled R.S.V.P. was a hoax after all. Mickey brought his foot down hard. How the glass smashed! Everyone could hear it. What a sign of wonderful luck. I sat waiting, patient as could be expected under the circumstances, in glad anticipation for my party to begin.

What a fool to think I'd get anything my way.

I acted like it was no skin off my nose, Nadine, you crashing down on us like a boulder from the heavens in the midst of your sister Electa's wedding, the most shining moment of my career. But it was murder, murder I tell you. If I hadn't worked my fingers to the bone on that reception I would have chased you down the aisle myself and wrung your filthy neck until you were dead. How did you get into the Ark in the first place? How did you fit there between the *Torahs*? Do you weigh nothing? Are you a *dybbuk* as I have insisted from the beginning? One of the possessed who changes from human form to animal or ghost by will? Did you become a tiny mouse in order to hide inside the holy of holies? Then, during the wedding ceremony, overtaken by the spirit of God, so strong on the *bima* of the synagogue, were you forced into your abomination of a woman's body which then fell upon us like a plague in the middle of what should have been the happiest day of my life?

I took your father's advice and became absolutely *shikker*. Did the guests have a good time? Frankly, I can't remember, although the phone rang off the hook with well-wishers the whole next day. No one, not even my mother or my sister Miriam, commented on the spectacle of the Ark. Too bad. I thought we created a new miracle: the synagogue did not instantly, upon your impact, crumble to the ground. I really expected Mickey's parents to demand an annulment. They are such religious people, and we have evil spirits in our family genes. But they swallowed whatever thoughts and judgments they held on the matter and went back to Boston. The next day they called to tell me that the event was lovely, the food was delicious, that both of them danced until they thought their feet would fall off.

Everyone applauded me. The neighbors, the cousins—my own mother actually admitted the party was grand. Even the rabbi had seen fit to ignore you, Nadine. But something was grabbing at my heart. It wasn't over yet, I could feel it. You had more evil deeds up your sleeve. I was sure of that, but I didn't know when you would strike. Suddenly it gripped me like a vice. *Rosh Hashanah*, the Jewish New Year. *Yom Kippur*, Day of Atonement. Was that not the time when the enemies of Israel fell upon us? What better time for you to defile us with your wickedness?

I was moved to protect our family from your foul presence, but I must be as crafty as you. If you could change form, you could sneak through any unclean opening. I must purify my home, make it sparkle so brightly that even you could not invade it with your insanity and filth.

I began with the closets. I pulled everything out—clothing, shoes, books, papers, room after room until each closet was empty and piles of family debris lay on floors throughout the house.

I found sheets of your violin music, published music that came from your lessons mixed with notebooks of compositions you created yourself. These I carried down to the basement and burned along with other evidence of you—your birth certificate, your medical records. I stopped short of the photographs because in order to destroy them I would have to burn up pictures of your sisters, of me and your father in happier times. I sealed the photographs in ziplock bags and stored them in the deep recesses of my linen closest, which I also had emptied and scoured.

I gathered up all of your old clothes and put them in piles. It occurred to me that I should give the clothes away to a charitable Jewish cause so that people less fortunate could have them, but they were cursed, as you were Nadine, and I wanted them out of my house and out of the world. Would I give the clothes to some poor unfortunate if they were contaminated with smallpox? Certainly not. The clothes must be buried at once as in the oldest days when people buried kosher dishes that had been touched by *traif*.

I bundled the garments up in an old sheet and carried them, like a body, to the woods behind our house. I dug a hole with a garden spade. The ground was soft and dry as the summer had been. I threw the clothes into the grave I had made. Then, like a dog, I buried them with my bare hands. To make certain none of your evil spirits would rise from your clothing to torture me again, I stomped on the grave with both feet until the ground beneath me was smooth and tight. I washed my hands under the spigot outside our house as I would upon returning from a funeral.

I came back into the house and tore the furniture apart, pulled it away from the wall, shook out and vacuumed the cushions. I pulled the books off the shelves and dusted them. I mopped and scrubbed, rubbed and polished, until everything sparkled. I made the house beautiful for the holidays. But more than that, I had protected us. There was no trace of you left. Knock at our doors! Come to our windows! Everything shone so brightly your own reflection would have scared you away.

Chapter 14

Just Desserts

My mother's house was too clean. There were flowers on the table and the holiday candles were already lit when we sat down for dinner. My father poured sweet wine into little goblets and made a *barucha*. We drank. We sipped our chicken soup, thick and golden, rich with salt. In each bowl swam three *kreplach*, three perfectly formed triangles of homemade dough filled with nearly identical little lumps of kosher hamburger. My mother cleared the table and brought forth *cholent*, brisket so tender it could melt in your mouth, with potatoes and carrots that had cooked with the meat for days. It was as if my mother had put her whole soul into the food for this New Year's feast. But there was no joy in this *Rosh Hashanah* dinner. Each mouthful was punctuated by heavy sighs from my grandmother, my Aunt Miriam, my mother and father, my Uncle Al. There was no other sound at the table but the slurping of soup and the cutting of meat, the sorrowful scraping of the best silver on the holiday china. Mickey and Electa were with Mickey's parents in Boston. There was no one with life in them to wake this party up. It was just like the old days before the wedding. I wished I were dead.

No one had mentioned Nadine or asked if I had seen her. In a way, I was relieved. Already I was tortured with the same dream every night: Chasidic men danced together, their sidelocks flying while crazed music played. Lesbians I knew from my women's studies classes swung each other wildly across the floor. I myself danced a jig with Kria who changed into my sister Electa and then Nadine. Every night in the dream Nadine held me close and then suddenly began to bark at me like a dog. Her lips drew back and she *was* a dog, snarling and snapping.

I'd swim up out of the dream, and like a worse nightmare, the real memories of the wedding came flooding back in jerky sequence: me in a bridesmaid gown. Nadine falling out of the Ark. Electa getting butch with everybody and ordering us to have the party anyway. Dancing, champagne, matzoh ball soup. Me in the mirror. More dancing. Finally Nadine jumping me in my own car on the way home.

First I was freaked out by her hijacking, and then I was furious. "What do you mean, take you to New Chelm?" I said. "You go in there right now and find Mommy and Daddy and apologize to them."

Nadine shook her head and made as if to get out of the car. All of a sudden I got worried that someone would see Nadine and me together and my mother would think I really did have something to do with Nadine's spectacular appearance. I decided not to argue and instead grabbed her by what was left of her vest. "Get in." I peeled out of the parking lot. Kria would have been proud of me. I think I left rubber.

We got all the way to the Mass. Pike entrance in silence. You could have cut the tension between us with a knife. I wanted to strangle Nadine, but that would take time and I needed to put as many miles between me and the rest of my family as possible.

Just outside of Ware I couldn't stand it any longer. "Nadine," my tones were measured, "how did you find out about Electa's wedding?" She looked in my direction, but her face was unreadable. "Someone broke into my apartment," I said, "was it you? Who told you where I live?"

Nadine stared out the window again. I thought I detected a shrug, but the fact was, I didn't even know if she could hear me. The whole rest of the way I started sentences I didn't finish, asked questions that were met with silence. "Where should I drop you off?" I asked as we at last crossed the bridge into New Chelm. I realized I had some fantasy that she didn't live in a house, that she camped out in the woods or slept on park benches. Nadine blinked, and I hoped she was going to talk to me at last. Please God, please, let us have a normal conversation! Instead, when I stopped at an intersection at the very edge of town, Nadine grabbed her knapsack and violin and jumped out of the car. I considered following her, but she'd already vanished into the inky darkness. I reached over and slammed the car door.

I wanted to worry about my own sister wandering around alone in the middle of the night, but by the time I pulled the car up and pushed myself, frilly dress and all, into my apartment, I was too furious to care. I ripped my dress off and threw it into a heap at the foot of my bed, then topped it with those stupid dyed-to-match pumps and my pantyhose. The whole thing looked like a giant melting ice-cream sundae. I lay in bed naked and closed my eyes. I had two sisters, a mother, a father, and if I wanted one, a lover. Feeling utterly alone, I cried myself to sleep.

The next day I had a disturbing thought. Maybe I should go over to the women's restaurant and find Nadine. Make peace. Bring her home and patch everything up. I had a fantasy that I could walk into the kitchen of the restaurant the back way and come upon Nadine standing there, her hair askew, an apron wrapped around her, chopping onions, frying them in a pan. "Psst," I would say, "Nadine!"

She would look up from her sizzling onions, wipe her hands on her apron, throw a greasy arm across my shoulder. Like an older sister, she would bring me out behind the restaurant. I'd offer her a cigarette. She'd take it. Together we would sit on the stoop and smoke. Then I'd brush a few stray hairs out of her eyes, run my finger over the ridges of her scar.

After our cigarettes, I would gather her up in my arms and force her to come home to my mother's house to repent. *Rosh Hashanah* and *Yom Kippur* were right around the corner. I could reunite Nadine with the rest of the family and be a hero to my people at last.

But here, in the middle of the most depressing New Year's dinner ever, I was glad I never had a chance to live my fantasy out. I never went to the restaurant to try to find her. Electa was with her new family, Nadine was disappeared. There wasn't a trace of her presence even here where we grew up. I was alone again in the house of the living dead. I loaded my plate with more brisket, potatoes, carrots, and beans. Suddenly I was starving.

I saw my parents less and less after that desolate *Rosh Hashanah*. *Shabbes* dinners became a time of stony silence. Without Electa to surprise and save us, it seemed hopeless. I tried a million ways to launch into cheery conversations about my life but every word I uttered about my professors or my academic achievements was met with dead eyes and the sound of scraping silverware. Once in a while my mother said, "That's very nice," between soup slurps. My father made no attempt whatever to feign interest. I never spoke about my personal or social life, even in code. The thought of a silence icier than the one I already faced was more than I could bear.

After *Shabbes* dinners my parents ritually viewed Electa's wedding pictures. This only depressed me further. Bad enough that I myself looked like a parody of a straight woman in that pink bridesmaid gown, that wasn't the worst part. The worst part was that we took in these photographs of false joy and enforced happiness in absolute silence.

No one ever mentioned the thing that had happened with Nadine.

How I longed for someone—my grandmother, my Aunt Miriam, even my father—to burst out, full of fake cheeriness, "Electa was such a lovely bride, and you were a beautiful brides-maid, Jane, and by the way, didn't Nadine look spectacular when she jumped out of the Ark and fell right on top of Mickey? I never realized how agile she was before it happened. You know, if they had Jews in the Olympics I bet she could try out."

But no one mentioned it, not even to say in their deadest zombie voices, "It was a *shandeh*, a shame of the highest order. We are so absolutely heartbroken we may not survive the winter."

That was how they acted. My mother and father, and when she was around, my Grandmother Minnie, sat like a family condemned to death. Finally I could stand it no longer. I stopped going home.

It helped that the winter was wild. The first big snow began on a Friday afternoon, and the roads were so bad my mother phoned to tell me not to come for *Shabbes*. After that, our routine was broken and I wasn't expected. It made me lonesome to leave them. I called them on the phone, but neither my mother nor father ever wanted to talk.

I imagined them frozen at the kitchen table mid-bite, as if some evil sorcerer had cast a spell. I would never be able to melt the icicles forming on their fingers and hands. Better to wait until the spring, which would warm them, maybe thaw their hearts or at least loosen their tongues so that they'd be able to speak.

I tried to focus on my life at school and on the fringes of the lesbian social scene in New Chelm. I cleaned test tubes, monitored biology experiments, and sat through interminable lectures on white male medical ethics which were not even close to my own. The only joy in my week came at two-fifteen every Tuesday and Thursday when I got to listen to Mia Zevin lecture on the politics of feminist spirituality. If my lab let out early, I might even get to class in time to find a seat next to Kria and hold hands. She and I had a standing date for coffee after class, and if Kria didn't have a meeting, and I didn't have an exam the next day, we'd go home together, make dinner, and spend the night.

My dream life was wrecked. In addition to the lesbian Chasids I was plagued with animated data sheets in which fact after medical and scientific fact danced through my brain, or I was subjected to an array of disconnected nightmares—bone yards, barbed wire, caverns full of dank water, crowded boxcars—none of which I could remember in any detail the next day.

Except for one, which began the first night of *Hanukkah*.

On the first night of *Hanukkah* I was on my belly in a line between two other women. We were crawling through what smelled like a sewer. We were tense and silent. I had a pistol in my hand. It seemed like we were crawling forever, and it was difficult because we were wearing long skirts. The woman ahead of me finally stopped and pushed a manhole cover up. I pushed her out of the hole, the woman behind pushed me, then I reached down and lifted her out. We ran toward a factory. Someone started shooting at us. The woman in front of me turned and shot back into the night. We kept running. We made it to the factory and pressed ourselves up against the wall. I opened my mouth to speak. The woman ahead of me covered my mouth with a gloved hand. I looked into her eyes. It was Nadine. I turned and found the other woman's face. It was my oldest sister, Electa.

This dream recurred at least once a week for months and left me exhausted, panicked, then ultimately resigned. Nights we spent together I fell asleep hugging Kria and had no dreams at all. I woke rested and replenished. But the other dreams exhausted me. I stopped eating, became pasty-faced and wan. The family curse had found me. Even though I never saw them, I was haunted by my family. I was to become one of the Morningstar living dead after all.

Chapter 15

A Life Among The Potato Heads

In certain ways it wasn't good that I lived alone and not in Vick Street anymore. At Vick Street, even though they were yelling at me all the time about my personal bad habits and private concerns, at least I was amongst other women. Up there, in that fancy apartment, I was in the lap of luxury, but I was sitting in it alone. With no one else to talk to, what else could I do, Nadine, but obsess about you? True, I did some dealing, so I had a few customers to keep me company. But face it, those women were all potheads and they didn't make such good companions once they were blotto.

When I went to sleep all I could remember was that I shared that soggy old water bed one and one time only, and with who, Nadine? You. I didn't change the sheets for weeks because they smelled like you. I still have some of your wild hairs I found in there. I keep them wrapped up tight, like wires, in the same magic box I use to save time capsule joints of my favorite pot, rocks from the Michigan Womyn's Music Festival, and other mementos of lesbianhood.

You still weren't at my house when I came home from work the day after you so spontaneously dropped from my window ledge onto my bed the night of your sister's wedding. I looked in the bathtub and under the bed, then went immediately to Vick

Street to find you. You weren't there either. Your door was unlocked and open about an inch. I could blow on it and the thing would swing all the way open. I pushed gently and crept into your room like a sneak thief. It didn't matter. There was nothing in there. Your violin was gone, your little stupid pile of clothes. Your mattress was still there, but it was all kind of kicked over to the side. The only thing left on the walls was this tacky xerox poster about lesbian-only events that was there before you even moved in. On the floor there were a couple of pieces of sheet music in your own handwriting, some balled-up Kleenex, and dust bunnies. It was pathetic.

I have to admit, I got somewhat hysterical and did something I'm not proud of. I was a woman in love and desperate, and I didn't have a clue, so I rifled through the drawers in your desk. But guess what? They were empty too. I was looking for a journal or one of those little locked diaries like I used to have when I was a kid, or even a random scrap of paper with a note on it. I wanted some kind of sign about where you were, something that said you had a master plan to rejoin your family or go off to furthest Asia Minor never to return. To tell you the absolute truth, what I really wanted was to find some shred of evidence that told what you felt about me, like was it true love or what, but there was nothing. I could see from the utter emptiness of the room that you were gone, really gone this time. I could imagine you hanging there from my bedroom window all I wanted. I could hope for you to be at my house, pray for it even, but the fact of the matter is, Nadine Pagan, you were gone from me and my heart was demolished.

Some weeks later, I went up to Willa Kaufman's land to take what was rightfully mine, that is, to harvest my pot. I didn't stop off at the cabin or the cliffs. I just went directly to my secret marijuana patch and pulled all my plants out by the roots. It's the way you're supposed to harvest pot, but it felt violent somehow, and that violence felt good. It was better than doing my second choice, which was to walk right into *Lechem V'Shalom* and break all the dishes because I was, very frankly, furious. Not just at you, either, but at all those buzz-cuts who threw me out of Vick Street and also the women at the restaurant who were getting on my case to quit being high when I came in to work. Could I help it if I kept burning things? It wasn't because I was high. It was because I had a broken heart. I've seen a few of them burn things when their lives weren't exactly going according to plan. Anyway, I pulled the plants and stuffed them, leaves down, into plastic trash bags. I had about twenty-five plants, full and beautiful. I shoved them all into the back seat of my bug, pulled off a flower top, rolled myself a joint, and drove back down those curvy-ass roads into New Chelm.

All of a sudden I had a thought. Maybe I could send you mental messages and you would get them and this would bring you back. I could be super specific and request not only your presence, but give you the idea that you really were in love with me big time. I could get books out of the library and figure out exactly how to do it. Lots of people knew how—Madame Blavatsky and Amy Semple McPherson to name only two. If those guys could do it, why couldn't I? My broken heart lightened, but with it still pounding in my hippie dyke chest, smiling and smoking, humming for the first time in days, I headed home. It was perfect. I was happy again at last.

I brought all the pot up to the apartment and for once, boy, I was glad again that I wasn't in Vick Street. I had a couple of nosy neighbors to watch out for, but that was nothing compared to the prying eyes of all those flat-tops. I just pretended I'd been to the Goodwill or something and hauled the bags up. Then I pulled the shades and hung the plants upside down in the bedroom closet so they could dry out. I figured they'd need a few weeks and then I'd be in business. There was enough stuff there to cover my living expenses and keep me buzzed for months. The plants smelled so good, you could about get loaded just standing in the doorway. I pulled a sticky flower top, grabbed a hit pipe and a pack of matches out of my utility drawer, and settled in at the kitchen table for some solitary meditation on astral projections, extrasensory perceptions, and general out-of-body lesbonic phenomena in order to better communicate with you, the missing Nadine Pagan.

I began by tinkering with the mind-blowing theory that I could will you back to me simply by getting so fucked up and sending out such strong vibrations that you'd have to come running. I held the smoke in as deep as I could and visualized you completely: your lunatic hair, your jagged scar, your insane asylum stare. Goddess, I wanted you. All of a sudden I realized I was supposed to be at work.

At first I was freaked out, but then I knew it didn't have to be so bad. I could make every minute of work a meditation and the point of that meditation would be you. What better place to try this than in a lesbian restaurant where everybody was talking to each other without opening their mouths half the time anyway.

When I walked into the restaurant I was about fifteen minutes late. Crystal shot me a dirty look. "I'm sorry," I said very sweetly. "I'm gonna do my best to be a responsible collective member from now on. Tell me what you want me to do." I was feeling feisty and excited about the world. With the conditions just right, I knew I could contact you, Nadine, no matter where you were. Crystal glared and sent me down to the basement to get some potatoes.

You know the setup down there. We have these big old storage bins with pounds and pounds of potatoes and pounds and pounds of onions on account of we are a lesbian collective and we buy from other lesbian farmer types and we try to economize. I would say, all told, there are about a million pounds of tuberous matter down there. I was fine for maybe ten seconds while I poked through the bins and loaded my apron up with spuds, but then the very, very weird thing that I wanted to happen happened.

All of a sudden, in the middle of all those damp and musty new potatoes and old onions, I swear to God, Nadine, I felt you. Like you were hiding out down there in one of those bins. I thought to myself, this is it, my ESP skills are working, she's really here. I was sure. But then I doubted myself. What if it was only an hallucination? But I felt you so strong I could practically taste you. I was positive you were buried alive right in the middle of the potatoes. So this is when I did the craziest thing so far. I started pulling all the potatoes out of the bin. Tossing them over my shoulders every which way until the whole bin was empty and I could see the pallet on the floor. Then I went for the onions, which I flung madly in all directions. But you weren't in that bin either. This is when I knew I must be out of my mind. You know that big, long food freezer in the basement? I opened it up and started chucking food out of that too, because if you weren't in the potato bin and you weren't under the onions, you had to be jammed in the freezer between big frozen vats of vegetable soup and marinara sauce.

I guess I was making quite a bit of noise or something because before I knew it, Crystal was down there with me, grabbing me by the shoulders. "Rose," she was shaking me, "what are you doing? Look at this mess!"

"Nadine is hiding down here. I know it!"

Crystal shot me a look like I was the biggest maniac on two feet and I thought, this is it, I'm the first lesbian feminist to be tossed out of a collective rooming house and lose her job at a collective restaurant in the herstory of the world. But what she did instead was take my hand and lead me upstairs. Then she sat me down at a table and put herself next to me. "Rose, Nadine isn't down in the basement. No one has seen Nadine for weeks." She touched my cheek and shook her head. "You look like hell."

There were no customers in the restaurant except one dyke way in the back room drinking a cup of coffee with a copy of *off our backs* spread in front of her. I felt safe all of a sudden the way I used to feel in the oldest days of women's restaurants and wimmin-only space and so I unburdened myself to Crystal. She looked so calm and sturdy sitting there, I couldn't understand why I broke up with her. Then I remembered I broke up with her because I was in love with you. It didn't matter. For the first time in about four years a flannel shirt on a shoulder looked like a comforting thing to cry on. I told her everything about me and you, Nadine—the last time I saw you, sex in the water bed, etc., etc. Crystal just sat there and didn't say much. When I was done she handed me a Kleenex and shook her head.

"Go home, Rose. Take the rest of the week off, just like you were sick. That is the sorriest story I've heard in a long, long time."

I checked out of *Lechem V'Shalom* and walked around New Chelm for a while, taking in the places I used to play with you, kind of looking for you in the laundromat, on the town commons, and through the woods all the way back up to my house. You weren't any of those places, Nadine, and nowhere did I feel the ghost of you the way I felt you down in the cellar with all those potatoes. I was desolate. You were gone from me forever. There was nothing left to do but go back to my apartment, get loaded, wash my sheets, and otherwise clean.

Chapter 16

Tashlich

Where was Nadine Pagan all this time? Everywhere you believed me to be. Only ask. Flame of the eternal light, weevil in the potato pile, I am our mother's worst fear, my lover's best fantasy. Like a good demon, I take many forms.

After our sister Electa chased me down the aisle of Temple *Beth Shalom* with athletic prowess above and beyond what any Morningstar daughter other than myself had previously demonstrated, I went back and hid in the bushes flat on my belly until the sounds of happy music drifted from the synagogue social hall. Then I found your lumpy old car, Jane, and hid in the back seat.

When at last I heard horns honking and cans clattering along the pavement, I poked my head up to see Electa and Mickey speed away in a car that said Just Married. Electa was driving. *Just* or *Only*, I wondered, and hunkered back down to my hiding place until you appeared.

I scared you but I didn't mean to. At other times I'd scared you worse. Poor Jane, human bucket brigade, pourer of water, savior of what is left of my strange thinking head. You asked me a million questions, but I sat silently, if you can call it that, my mind racing with all I wanted to tell you. There was too much, and all I could do was look at your face, then look away as you stared into mine. Yours was a grief-stricken face, smeared with paint and fury. What cracked words out of my bloody mouth could soothe you? I could stand it no longer and jumped ship. Vanished into the night. Ran for my life. Who was chasing me? Not you. Not Electa. You had already come after me and given up. Nor was I fleeing from our mother whose arms were overflowing with lit matches and kerosene of her own to add to my personal pyre. No, devils were chasing me. Little demons so tiny no human could see them. They sat in my ears and sang to me. They crawled up my neck and pulled at my hair. They slid down my spine and into my legs. They offered to set me on fire again, and so I flew into the night. Whenever I rested they hung on me like flies.

I found my lover Rose. I have my ways. I scratched and whined at the ledge of her window like a dog until she let me in. Then she bathed me and fed me and I paid her back with sex. I tried to sleep but little bee demons stung me all over. Quiet as anything I rolled out of bed. I stole one of her T-shirts and one of her vests, but I kept my own jeans even though they stank. Then I slipped out the bathroom window, shinnied down the back porch, and snuck through the woods to Vick Street. I crawled up the rooming house fire escape and broke into my own room. The demons were singing to me, so I stuffed everything I could into my knapsack and ran out the way I came. There was no place to go to escape them. They only stopped while I was running. I ran. It was getting light. I didn't know where to go so I ran to the restaurant. There was a loose basement window around the back. I pushed it open and dropped my knapsack down, then squeezed my way in. I reached up through the open window and pulled my violin to me. Then I pulled the window shut behind me and sank into darkness.

It was cool there and quiet. I went around behind the bins of potatoes and onions and slept until I heard feet stomping and pots clanging. The phone rang. Muffled voices spoke. The floor creaked overhead, the basement door opened. Someone came down the stairs, poked around in the bins, then trod back up again.

No one suspected my hiding place. The buzzing inside me stopped. How many days passed? How many hours? I slept and woke, woke and slept, ate raw potatoes like a mouse, peed in the sink like some hobo. Who knows how long I lived this way until the evil spirits buzzed inside again. I could stay still no longer. I waited until it was stone silent and pitch black inside the restaurant and out of it, then I pushed through the window the way I had come and ran into the night.

I was driven by that never-ending buzzing. What were they telling me, those demons? Out in the air as I ran, it came clear. The whole long way as I walked on achy legs and throbbing feet I saw Mickey Robbins stepping hard on the wedding glass and our sister Electa falling deep into his arms. I saw the flames I made out of the two of them together as I trampled on their holy union. I felt our mother at my back, breathing down my neck, her rage burning into me like branding irons, and so I ran. The whole long way, as I traveled on unsteady feet down the middle of Main Street, up onto the highway, and under the light of the moon, kicking at pebbles on back roads, pulling down branches, tripping over roots and stones, I knew now what was chasing me. Why did I do it? Hide in the Holy Ark and pose as a *Torah*? Whatever possessed me, or who?

Night turned to morning, and still I saw Mickey's foot and still there was the smell of the *Torah*, soft and velvet in my nose, and still I could not force these things together to make sense. I hiked up a dirt road, into a birch forest, past rocks as big as Lot's wife. I carried the clothes on my back and my beloved violin. After many hours of chasing myself, through some miracle of navigation, I found myself on Willa Kaufman's land in the country.

I found the tiny cabin and pried the padlock off with a strong branch. I closed the door behind me, wrapped myself in a big red blanket, fell back onto the narrow cot, and cried. I cried until my teeth ached and my eyes were red and swollen, and then I slept without dreaming, I do not know for how long. When I woke it took me some minutes to remember where I was, and then I cried again.

For the next days I sat without moving. Barely did I breathe.

Barely did I mark when the sun came up and when it went down again. Chickadees appeared at the cabin window and sang to me, but did they bring me pleasure? No. When I absolutely had to, I went outside the cabin and peed, but I did not linger and never did I venture into the deepest woods.

Then one morning I woke to a new season on the land. The air was crisp and cool, the sun hung lower in the sky. I pulled the blanket close around me and walked out of the cabin down toward the river that crossed the land. The water ran swiftly. I dipped my hands in and drank and drank. I washed my face in the chilly waters, but when I saw the reflection of my own face I barely knew who I was. I howled like a dog, like a wolf, because I had become one. *Vildeh chei-eh!* I had made of myself a wild animal! My face in the water was proof of this. What was there left to do but howl?

As if to put myself out, I, Nadine Pagan jumped into the river and swam, first to one side and then to the other, again and again, side to side, until I could swim no longer. I dragged myself out of the river, wet and shivering, and trudged back to the cabin. I peeled my clothes off and left them to bake dry in the early autumn sun.

When I slept, I dreamed the dog catcher was after me. When I woke, I searched for food. The days went by and the days went by, and on the night of the new moon I had this dream:

I take a knife and with my right hand I slice off my left-handed fingers one by one. These I place in a big black kettle. With my bloody stump I hold an onion, with my right hand I chop; with my stump I hold a carrot and this I also chop. I slice I dice I rice I chop stalks of celery, cloves of garlic, green beans, and tomatoes. These I throw into the pot with my fingers and begin to make soup, which I stir with a wooden spoon on an open flame. When it bubbles from boiling I ladle it into wooden bowls. In each bowl I am careful to put a finger, and of these bowls I give one to you, Jane, one to Electa, one to Rose. The biggest bowl, the one with my thumb in it, I give to our mother who is at the head of the table saying a blessing over the candles. Our Zaideh Yitzhach is on the ceiling playing a fraïlich. *"Why is she lighting the candles?" I whisper. No one answers. Instead they sit, each of them smacking their lips, eating me alive. "But why is she lighting the candles?" I whisper again.* Zaideh Yitzhach *jumps down from the ceiling and pats my stump gently. "Happy New Year," he tells me, "It's* Rosh Hashanah."

I woke sweating and moved not a muscle. I counted the days as best as I could remember from my days as a *Torah* to my days as a rotten potato to my current days as a werewolf. Our *zaideh* was right. It was the Jewish New Year, *Rosh Hashanah.* I must go down to the river and let go my sins. I took with me my violin, a charred stick, and a scrap of paper I found under the stove. I pulled on my shoes and to the river I walked.

At the water's edge I scratched the words, the home, *ha bayit*; the fire, *ha esh*; the family, *ha mishpacha*, and these I threw into the river. I took from my pocket the few dollars I had, and these I threw into the river as well. From my violin case I lifted my music notebook, which I had filled over time with stories and lies. This, also, I threw into the river, and with it my guilt, my shame, the sound of our mother's voice. I picked out little pieces of lint and balled-up cookie fortunes, thirty-seven cents in pennies and dimes. All of this I tossed and watched as it drifted, sunk, and spun on the choppy waters flowing south. On an old playing card, the three of spades, I wrote your name, Jane, and then Electa's. This I threw into the river and after that the charred stick, my pen.

But having divested myself of all my goods, I felt no better than I had before. I thought to throw my violin to the waters, but an unseen hand stopped me. This violin was a gift to me from our Grandmother Minnie and before that a gift to her from our Great-Grandpa Yitzhach and was not mine to throw away. It reminded me of our entire family and all I could not be to them, and so I could not throw this into the water at my feet. I sat on the bank and watched the river flow, gentle waves lapping on muddy shores. "All my life drifts before me, and after me who will stand up for me, who will love me after all I have done?"

Thus, in the chill of late September, in this spot in the woods where summer's smell still lingered, I untied those heavy boots which had carried me so faithfully from one spot to another and stood them by the river. I took off my socks and these I tossed into the water. I unzipped my jeans, climbed out of them, and these I threw in also, and then Rose's matted vest, my tattered shirt and cotton underpants, and finally the T-shirt I had stolen from Rose, until I stood naked and shivering at the water's edge.

And for the sin of not knowing how to put a hot fire out in my own head, for the sin of mingling with *Torahs* and falling on family, for the sin of not knowing when to stop, I threw myself into the river, leaving behind that sweet violin brought with love and care by an old man I never met to this country so long ago. And I, Nadine Pagan, fell into the river, so sweet and yellow, how warm as it carried me down down into the deep of it, the sweet water tumbling over me as I fell down down down.

Part 3

Chapter 17

The Mysterious Disappearing Girl

I fly and then I stop flying, the weight of my body in the swift river pulls me down and down through the water into the river bed, in slowest motion, through layer after layer of clay and sand, muck and mire, I push I push, pebbles and shells stick in my mouth, I'm dead I know it, but wait . . . I breathe.

Fingers pull my ankles, hands grasp my hands, some magnet draws me down down down. My neck is breaking, my lungs are collapsing, twigs and leaves lodge in my throat. I am thrust farther, my cheeks fill with pebbles, my nails pack with clay, I scratch the sediment walls as I am carried down down, butt first, hair streaming like tendrils behind me, certain I'm a dead person, a conscious corpse, drawn deeper and deeper into the cool, sticky mud.

Suddenly, the mud breaks. Waters rush past me, and I am carried on the crest of a wide wave to a limestone grotto where I choke and cough up water and bilge, where I spit out small stones and dead leaves, then breathe real air at last.

I sink down feet first and my toes touch slippery rock, solid ground. I am up to my shoulders in warm, gentle water. I swim, then walk, toward shore.

A woman is waiting, naked, round-muscled. Her breasts are large, her shoulders wide, her eyes are brown and golden. This woman at the water's edge, my height, no taller, a head full of wild red hair, holds her hands out to me as I slip and slide on the grotto floor. I want to resist her, swim the other way, but find I cannot. I am heavy here and cannot run. I do not know the lay of the land.

"Come," says the woman, who lights the way with a lantern, "follow me quickly. We have much to do."

I am unsteady on the limestone floor. I cannot run. I glance down at my feet. Someone has tied salt boxes to them with rags. My legs are also wrapped with rags, and the floor of the cave is now covered with icy snow which cracks and bites into my feet and ankles with each tiny step. I am no longer naked. I wear a heavy cloth coat, bulky, two sizes at least too big. On my head, what's this, a little cap, and long *payism* brush against my cheeks. *Tzitzis* hang down to my waist. I am a little Jewish boy in the middle of nowhere. I am not alone.

All around me walk people dressed as I, some older, some younger, some women with shawls on their shoulders, some men carrying bundles, some have real shoes on their feet and some only rags. "Where are we going?"

The woman who met me wears now a long white beard, a wide-brimmed hat, a wool coat. She touches a finger to her wrinkled lips. "These woods are full of danger." She leads the way through crusty snow to a clearing. In the middle of it, sticking up out of the snow, is a heavy wooden door made from rough-hewn boards. A big rusted ring is the handle. The stranger and some other men pull the door open. "Climb down."

All the people do as they are told, all but me, who hesitates on the edge and peers into the cellar. "Get in, little boy," the old man tells me, "God will protect you." I stare into the old man's eyes. He looks like Electa. "It's safe, be a good boy, climb in."

What choice do I have? I drop down onto the ladder. The old Electa man follows and pulls the door closed behind us. Then two more men come and bang it shut with nails.

Here in the underground chamber torches hang on damp walls. Children like me huddle around women whose heads are covered with dusty kerchiefs. Some of the women weep, some sing, others stare into space silent. There are a few men, very old, who sit along the walls and bob their bearded heads over prayer books and chant.

There are no windows, no doors. I glance around, not frantic but helpless. There is no one I know here, surely no one I trust. I have no family. I belong to no one. Everyone looks like someone I saw through the crack in the Ark at Electa's wedding, but no one knows who I am. I start to cry.

Then a woman holds out a piece of black bread to me, and a ladle full of water. "Little boy, little boy, eat this. We may be trapped here for the rest of our lives, but at least you'll be big and strong." I take the bread. "Momma?"

She shakes her head. "I'm not your mother."

I stare at her again. She looks exactly like Fay. It makes me feel sad.

"These are my children," the woman says. She puts her arms around the sleeping bundles at her sides. "Come sit by us, it's warmer that way. You have to rest when you can. You never know when you'll have to start running again." The woman pats the space between herself and her babies. I am exhausted and curl into it, grateful. I fall fast asleep, the piece of black bread still in my hand.

When I wake I am starving. I look for the black bread, gift of the one who looks like our mother, but I am naked now, no hands full of bread. I dip my head instead into the river rushing all around me and swallow what I can. Someone taps my shoulder. I turn. Who's there? Neither the old Electa man nor the stranger who met me at the grotto, not our mother nor her double nor any of the people, women or men, from the chamber underground. In fact, all of those people have disappeared. No, before me stands a woman, short and familiar, with eyes like yours, Jane. She stands with her hands extended, holds out a red blanket like the one I left on Willa Kaufman's land. "We have been waiting for you, Nadine. Follow me."

135

The other woman is not naked, wears jeans and a sweatshirt, sturdy shoes on her feet. I envy her. I'm cold and my feet hurt. She leads the way with a flashlight as we walk along the water's edge. At a place where the banks narrow, she jumps lightly to the other side. She offers me her hand, and instead of running the other way, which is what I want to do, I take it eagerly and jump to meet her.

"It turns to dirt here. You'll feel leaves and mud under foot. Be careful not to snag your toes."

I walk gingerly behind her. She is sure and steady, but me, I slip and slide. If only I had not left my shoes by the river. "Just over this ridge and we're halfway there." She holds me by the elbow and guides me on the rocky path.

At the top of the ridge the woman with your eyes aims her flashlight straight ahead and blinks it on and off. From out of the darkness, three dots of light return.

There is the faint sound of oars pushing gently through the water. You flash your light again and three stronger dots answer. Soon a small boat appears. Someone who looks just like Rose is at the helm. "Get in," she says, "quickly. Don't say a word."

I take my place in the back of the boat, feel down to my sore toes. Once again they are wrapped in rags. Once again I am wearing a little cap and a giant overcoat. The woman with your eyes and Rose are now very old women, stooped, wrapped in shawls and *babushkas*. Old Rose moves her lips slowly, just a whisper above the *whoosh whoosh* of oars.

The little boat slides through the darkness and in time we reach the other side. The old women hitch up their skirts and step out. Deftly they pull the boat to shore. While the woman with your eyes ties the vessel up, Old Rose throws me over her shoulder. "Be very still. We're trying to pass you off for a sack of potatoes."

I giggle.

"Be serious." Old Rose is stern. "Pretend you're a sack of potatoes and we can slip past. Otherwise, I can't be responsible."

Remembering my life in the potato bins back at *Lechem*

V'Shalom it is easy to comply. I go limp in the old woman's arms and she carries me down a street that smells of onions and tar, of salt from the sea.

Both old women walk stooped over, speak neither to each other nor to me, nor for that matter, to anyone else. Their pace is grandmotherly, but the arms that hold me are comforting and even strong.

At last they stop in front of a tumble-down house that sags under its own weight. The woman with your eyes knocks. The door creaks open. Someone who sounds just like Grandmother Minnie answers. "You've got the child?"

"This sack of potatoes."

"Bring him in. You weren't followed?"

The door is bolted. Old Rose—and is it Jane?—take off their shawls but keep their *babushkas* tied to their heads. Someone unwraps my rags and rubs my feet. It *is* Grandmother Minnie. "You're a good boy, very brave," she touches my cheek.

Old Rose sets a piece of honey cake and glass of sweet wine at my side. "You've had a dangerous night. This will help you sleep." She swaddles me in a soft blanket and lays me like a baby on a mat of rags by the stove.

"Not the most comfortable bed, but at least you'll be warm. Eat now," they tell me, and each one kisses my face.

Before I swallow half the honey cake I am fast asleep.

I, Nadine Pagan, wake in a place where the stench is human, human refuse, burning humans, humans rotting alive in their own shit and blood. On my feet, wooden clogs which scrape against my bones. I wear a dress made out of wet cardboard. In the rain, as I stand now, the dress is heavy and heavier. My shoes stick deep into the mud. I have no hair, my eyeballs bulge.

I pick through a garden of human fertilizer. I sweep the bones from a giant oven, push them out, gag and remember that one of these sets of bones was a sister, a mother, an aunt. In another part of this desecrated planet a father is dying, a brother-in-law. I sweep, I cry, I make this lament:

My bones your bones
all of them the same bones
I'll shovel them up
until I drop
then someone other
will shovel up mine.
My bones your bones
in a minute I'll drop.

I wake up on a plush velvet couch. I hear the *scratch scratch* of pen to paper, see bent over a small writing table the back of a woman with hair very dark and curly, piled high on her head and tied with a ribbon. She is wrapped in a shawl, a candle bums at her side. Through a closed door I hear the muffled voices of more women talking. For a minute I think I am in the back room of *Lechem V'Shalom.*

"Excuse me." My voice is so clear and strong I surprise myself. "What place is this?"

The woman writing finishes her sentence, then turns to me. "Rest quietly, Nadine. I'll get you some tea."

"Where am I?"

The woman comes to my bedside and touches my forehead with the palm of her hand. "Rest, darling Nadine, soon all questions will be answered." I study her while she walks away, this woman in a black silk dress. Who is she and what am I doing here on a couch in a satin bathrobe, a fire in the fireplace, women talking in another room? I watch the shadows from the kerosene lamp flicker on the ceiling. I feel like I've been run over by a truck. When I try to lift myself off the couch, I can barely move my head.

The woman in black comes back with a little teapot and a china cup. She puts them down on the night stand and tucks the blankets around me.

I try to speak again but the muscles in my throat close. The woman pours tea and holds it to my mouth. Steam envelops me.

"My name is Magda," the woman says. I swallow the tea. "I live here with my three sisters. We are very glad to see you alive.

Some of us wondered if you'd even make it. You must rest now and recover quickly. There is much to be done and many women wish to talk with you." Magda holds my head as she lays the pillows flat against the couch and gently lowers me down. Then she turns the kerosene lamp out and I sleep.

I am in a boxcar jammed between dozens of other people. I can hardly move. I can pee in a tin can if I want to, but it doesn't matter, the whole place smells terrible. Someone is puking in one corner. In another corner someone died two days ago and no one is doing anything about it. We've been traveling like this for days and nights, how many no one even knows.

Some father puts his arm around my shoulder. The train rumbles on. I can hardly breathe. I fall asleep against some mother's leg.

It is blue sky morning. I am in a deck chair on the porch of a cottage by the sea. I am wrapped in a wool blanket. In this light Magda looks like our mother as she pulls a square table up by my side. Her sister, Esther, whose hair is wild and red, follows with a tray full of breakfast. A third sister, Shula, who looks like our grandmother, drags out two chairs. I sit up and take notice. I want to run away.

"So look at her, she's a regular wide-awake woman!" a fourth woman says. "I'm Etta. You're looking good." She looks a little like you, a little like Electa, as she pours tea from a gleaming copper pot into each of our cups.

"These are your sisters?" I ask Magda. Everyone wears clothes from a different time. Do they really look like people I know?

Esther produces a deck of cards and a box of tiny cigars.

"Not before breakfast," Magda/our mother says.

"Why not?"

"We have company."

"Who's company? This is how I am in real life, Nadine. I smoke before breakfast and in the old days, once or twice I lost my shirt in a poker game. Before breakfast."

"She doesn't know from the old days."

"Don't you?"

"She has no idea what you're talking about," Etta says with a wave of her hand, "In the meantime, the food is turning to ice."

"So you won't play cards."

"Ask her later, Esther."

"Later, Esther, she says." Esther tucks the cards into a drawer, but she doesn't extinguish her cigar. "How do you like the tea, Nadine? I brewed it myself, the Russian way. You're very cute." She brushes my cheek with her hand. "Maybe you'll have some fun with me one of these days."

The other sisters roll their eyes. They fill my plate for me and watch me eat. As I spoon up mouthfuls of egg and black bread, the waves roar gently, gulls fly, the sisters talk among themselves.

I stuff my face and look from one to the other. Do I know what they are talking about, or who? "Where are we?"

"This is our house."

"But it's not the same house I was in last night, and you may or may not even be the same women who brought me here—" My voice is clear and strong. It pleases me to speak.

Etta leans over and pats my hand. "It's good you've come, Nadine. Don't be confused. Things change here often. Sometimes you will wake in a different bed than the one you fell asleep in. Sometimes you will feel like somebody else entirely. But don't worry. Someone is always sure to recognize who you are."

"Incidentally," Esther says, "I was at your sister Electa's wedding. Lovely affair, didn't you think?"

I choke on my tea. The other women huddle around me and pat me on the back. "I didn't mean to upset you."

When I get my breath again I look at Esther carefully. "I ruined the wedding—"

Esther waves me away. "Nah—"

"I ruined the wedding and that's what killed me—"

"Killed you? Nadine, darling, you're not dead!"

"I'm not?"

"No," says Esther, "of course you aren't. Nadine, my darling, you're merely underground.

Chapter 18

They Do It With Mirrors

Fall turned into winter and it was a long winter, let me tell you. I went back to work at *Lechem V'Shalom*, but I had to swear on a stack of lesbian spiritual guides that I would absolutely never ever come to work loaded again. Did that mean just loaded, or that I got loaded an hour before I came to work, or wouldn't get loaded until work was over? It didn't matter. I just never got high on my way to work anymore, and if I did, I was careful not to let it show.

Crystal went out of her way not to ask me to go down to the basement again, which was a good thing because it still spooked me. It wasn't just the basement, either; it was everywhere in the restaurant. I'd see some shadow or hear some rustling in the bushes, a glass would break, a fork would drop—and I swear to God, Nadine, it was you.

I got all these books out of the library about astral projection and out-of-body experiences and near-death experiences and really-died-then-came-back-to-life experiences. I even took an all-day workshop called *Finding the Out-of-Body Lesbian Within*, which was led by some dyke who swears she was the Queen of Babylonia in a past life. I didn't buy it. The workshop was just a lot of lying on the floor and breathing heavy. I fell asleep during the past-life regression part, so I didn't get too much out of it, although I did learn from this Queen of Babylonia that the key to positive out-of-body experiences was ritual and routine. So that was how I did my winter. I developed a routine. I worked at the women's restaurant, I sold dope, I smoked dope, and I sat for hours at my kitchen table with a red candle going, trying to conjure you up. And I will say one thing, I had some of the best dreams I have ever had in my life during that period, none of which I can remember. I really should have written them down, but you know how it is—you never have a pen in your bed when you need it.

There were two other things that were part of my ritual that winter: number one, making soup at home. Even though I did it for a living, it was quite satisfying to chop and sauté and simmer and boil while the snow fell all around me. Number two was I really got into cleaning. One day, after I sold about three ounces and was feeling fat moneywise, what do you think, did I go to the Tell My Horse wimmin's bookstore and buy a shitload of records or a stack of magazines and books? No way. I went to Caldor's and bought a pair of yellow rubber gloves and a white plastic bucket and about a zillion sponges, a giant bottle of Lestoil, three cans of Comet, some Windex, two rolls of paper towels, and dug in and started cleaning.

It made sense because, boy, I'd been living in that place since the end of the summer and I hardly lifted a finger in the cleaning department. I mean, the ring around the bathtub could have been an art exhibit in the Guggenheim, I'm not kidding. There were seeds and roaches of the marijuana type everywhere, and life-size dust bunnies burrowed in every imaginable surface. The dish count in the sink was not going to win me a *Better Homes and Gardens* award either. It was about two days before my period. I lined up all my cleaning products on the kitchen table, then started with the bathtub because that was the grodiest, and I just cleaned and cleaned and cleaned—rub, scrub, mop, scour, swab, etc. I didn't even know I had it in me, one room at a time, cleaner and cleaner, more and more organized, until there wasn't one speck of dust, not one piece of paper out of place. I washed the windows and I washed the curtains—I mean we are talking about the world's cleanest lesbian home here and I'm not even a Virgo.

That was my morning ritual. In the evenings I'd come home from the restaurant and take a bath. I'd put on this record of violin music you gave me the first year I knew you. I'd light a candle, pull out my fancy dope box, sit down at the kitchen table, and pack my hit pipe. Then I'd smoke it and meditate on you. I even wrote you letters in my journal. Dear Nadine, they would say, even if you don't want to come to me in person, please please, enter my dreams. I await you tonight under the moon and stars, yours with love and devotion, Rose.

Most nights, no matter how clean my apartment was, I never actually got to you. Once or twice I found myself rowing a boat in some dark cove or dancing with a bunch of dykes from another country. I was sure that if I remained vigilant, I would find you through the stratosphere. It just had to be.

It might have gone on like that forever, but then my labor and toil in the lesbian cosmos came to fruition at last. The weird thing was, I wasn't even high when it happened. I had Patti Smith blasting and was in the middle of polishing the bathroom mirror. This so happened to be my all time favorite morning cleaning task. Windex jazzed me right up. It's better than coffee for a first-thing-in-the-morning buzz. So there's Patti wailing, *Because the night belongs to lovers/because the night belongs to love*, and me, I am going round and round on the smooth silver surface, around and around, trying like crazy to get the streaks out, polishing and polishing, when all of a sudden *my hand goes into the mirror*. Dig it. Not through the glass like I broke it, but *into the actual surface of the mirror*. Like I could feel my hand but I couldn't see it. I pinched myself with my other hand to make sure this wasn't one of my disrememberable dreams, but it hurt. I was awake alright, and I was up to my wrist in the bathroom mirror.

I pulled my hand out. It was whole. I still had a crumpled up paper towel in it and everything. I thought, boy, the residual high on that sinsemilla I grew was stronger than I figured. I put my fingers on the mirror again and pushed. This time I went in up to my elbow. I pulled my arm out. I was amazed.

I put on some hippie lesbo music, and even though it was daytime, I lit a candle. I brought the candle to the kitchen and sat at the table. Where did the path into the mirrors go? Could I get all of myself in there? There was a full-length mirror on the closet door in the bedroom. I brought the candle over there and pressed my finger tips against it. Into the mirror they went. I pulled my hand out real quick and sat down on the floor.

What did it mean? What did it mean that I could stick my hand into a mirror not once but any time I wanted to? Obviously it meant that I was supposed to go all the way in and do . . . what? Maybe if I climbed all the way into the mirror I'd find you, Nadine. Then again, what if I got stuck in the fourth dimension like in that "Twilight Zone" episode where the little girl gets trapped in the closet. She yells, "Help me, help me!" and her parents can see her but they can't get near her. Boy oh boy. I sure wished I hadn't fallen asleep during that past-life regression with the Queen of Babylonia. I blew the candle out and went to the restaurant to work.

That night I had a very scary dream. I was standing naked on the edge of some cliff and below me was the ocean. I was suspended in air, my arms just kind of floating at my sides, in a cave of light. Behind me I could hear some women and old guys praying. They were all wrapped up in these white silk shawls with fringes, rocking and crooning. Little kids were sleeping and dancing. Remnants of yellow stars were sewn to everybody's coat sleeves.

I looked down at my feet. I was wearing these funky wooden shoes. Then I noticed I had on this gray coat that was so heavy it made my shoulders stoop. The praying stopped without warning, and all I could hear was sobbing. There was barbed wire everywhere and the smell of people being cooked like cows.

In my body I was Rose alright, but also this really old woman.

144

I wasn't old in years, but my breasts were shriveled, my ribs stuck out, my fingers were all bony and gnarled. I tried to talk, but one by one all the teeth fell out of my head.

Then I was walking along some grassy path. I was wearing sandals. I had this incense ball that was smoking up a storm hanging off a chain. And get this—I was dressed like a nun. Me, a nun! There were a dozen women just like me standing ahead of me on line. Behind me were a dozen more. We were all chanting in Latin and walking up away from the ocean. Behind us there was a rowboat paddling back to a really big ship with masts and sails and everything. We walked together up this rocky path. It was very steep. Just ahead of us was that same cave of light. I was floating there, in the mouth of the cave, beckoning myself and all the other nuns in. Finally, close up to me, so real and close I didn't think I was dreaming, came your Nadine Pagan face. You were talking to me real loud, right in my ear, but I couldn't understand you. "What are you talking about? What do you want me to do?" I yelled so loud I woke myself up.

I lay in bed sweating. It was still dark out. I was due in at the restaurant in a few hours, but I was so exhausted it was like I never slept at all. "When are you going to jump in and do it?" I asked out loud. I heard myself answer, "Right now."

I unplugged the telephone and turned off all the lights. I didn't know if I should do this with or without clothes because you never knew when you were walking through a mirror where you were going to end up or what the weather would be like. Was it winter in there like it was out here or what? I put on my good hiking boots and decided to wear layers just like at the Michigan festival because I could always take clothes off but if I didn't have a flannel shirt when I needed one it was tough shit. Also, I put a bunch of stuff in my knapsack that I might need like a flashlight, some clean underwear, my journal with a couple of pens, my tarot cards, a red candle, and an extra pack of matches. I debated with myself a long time about whether or not to bring pot. I didn't think they had customs inside my particular mirror, but it would be pretty terrible to get all the way in and then be sent back because I had drugs, or even worse, thrown in the mirror slammer. Also, something told me this was one of those rare things that was better done straight. What I did was roll one skinny little flower top joint and stick it in the bottom of my left boot.

It was about three in the morning by the time I lit my white candle and amber incense and stood at the mirror on the closet door. I have to admit I looked pretty hot, like really, my best lesbian self. My hair was perfectly braided into a little skinny tail at the back of my head, my blue flannel shirt was tucked smartly into my favorite jeans, a little shell dangled from my left ear.

I closed my eyes and breathed slowly, put my left hand against the mirror and pushed. In it went. Then I stepped forward with my right foot. I pushed my face in next. It was very cold, like walking into a meat locker at first and pitch black. It occurred to me that it wasn't such a good idea to leave a candle burning in my apartment so I picked it up with my left hand and brought it in with me. That was it, I was inside and moving like on a conveyor belt or something, only there was nothing under my feet except air. *Whoosh*. I was kind of flying at a reasonable rate of speed standing up. It was very interesting, especially when I was doing it sideways or on my back. The candle kept burning.

For a long time it was like that, me *whoosh whooshing* through this weird airstream with these eerie echoes of sounds I couldn't make out bouncing all around me. It was like bunches of different people muttering in bizarre languages from every direction. Frankly, the novelty began to wear off after about an hour. I was getting pretty bored. Then all of a sudden I landed—not on my ass either, but standing up like a cat. I hardly lost my balance or anything. *Whoosh*, like sliding into first base, I'm standing on this limestone ridge. There's all this water rushing every which way and don't ask me why, I just start walking along this river like I know where I'm going. Right away I'm not walking alone anymore, I'm not even on that ridge anymore, I'm tromping through the snow with a bunch of other people. I'm this older woman now, about forty years old, I got these funky shoes with kind of high heels on and this old cloth coat with a fur collar and I'm walking at the end of some big crowd of people. No one is saying anything. I don't have any socks on, I have silk stockings and my feet are freezing. Somebody's grandma with a funky scarf around her head asks me in this weird language to help her carry this big valise she's got. I just ignore her and pretend like I don't understand what she's saying but really I do. Next thing I know an old guy in a black hat with a big beard is hurrying us along. Then I am climbing down this ladder into a big stone room wearing high heels, if you can believe it, and trying to find some place to sit down where I won't get my coat dirty. I'm dying for a cigarette. A man with this goofy fedora and a brown beard is puffing away, but when I go over to bum one from him he looks in the other direction and won't give me the time of day.

Finally I spot this redhead in a really hot outfit—navy suit, hose with seams up the back, little hat with a veil, fur coat over her shoulders, one foot up on her suitcase, the whole bit. She's smoking and talking to some guy in a suit, but when I catch her eye she winks at me. I saunter over and notice we're in a train station, not a cave, and not only that, but we all have yellow stars sewed to our coats, including these little kids who are running around playing. Then these soldiers come in and start calling off names. One by one the waiting room starts to empty out and before I know it, this redhead has her arm through my arm and she walks me to the door. As soon as we're out on the platform, *bam*, we start running like madwimmin. I'm in jeans again with my good boots on my feet.

Don't ask me how this happened, but the next thing I know I'm in this monastery or something, walking arm in arm with the redhead, only now we're both dressed up like nuns, just like in my dream. The funny thing is, it doesn't occur to me to talk to her or ask her any questions or anything. I just kind of figure we're walking around this garden for a reason and she knows

147

what it is even if I don't and sooner or later she'll get me to you, Nadine, although I never asked her if she could.

Suddenly we're walking down a hallway, our shoes *click clicking* against a stone floor. Then we're in some rowboat. Then she's not even in it with me anymore, I'm just rowing this boat by myself. Someone is flashing a light at me and I'm flashing one back. When I get to the other side there's a dyke that looks kind of familiar standing there and who has she got with her—you! Only not you as I understand you, Nadine. You're you dressed up like a little boy. In fact you are a little boy and you look totally lost and confused. This other dyke puts you in the boat and climbs in behind you. Then off we go rowing, *splash splash*, but not speaking, *splash splash*, into the unknown night.

All of a sudden I wake up and I'm dancing cheek to cheek with that redhead, the very weird thing being that both of us are women—I mean dressed like women, girly women. She's playing with my hair and kissing my neck, and I've got my hand on her butt and it's getting sort of steamy, I mean she can lead better than anyone I've ever danced with in my life. It's sort of turning me on. It takes everything I've got to remember what I'm doing here. "You haven't seen Nadine Pagan anywhere have you?"

She leans into my ear and says in this sexy voice, "Of course I have. I'll take you there as soon as this dance is over."

Then before I know it we're in this jazzy roadster with the top down cruising at very high speeds, then we're on this horse, then we're in a boat again, and eventually I'm sitting at some ancient kitchen table dressed again (thank *God*) in my jeans and flannel shirt. Red is now wearing this very hot shiny green dress with a bustle on her butt and she's pouring some tea out of this big copper teapot into a glass. There's some other woman in a black dress hanging out in a corner reading a book and there, right across from me, wearing one of my old T-shirts which I hadn't been able to find for about three months, and a pair of overalls, was you, Nadine Pagan. Only your face was completely clear. No purple scar, not even a trace of it. Your eyes were open and bright

148

and your hair was still long and curly but was sitting around your face in a somewhat organized fashion. I was a goner, but I tried to keep cool. "So," I said, "how ya been?"

You wouldn't say anything, just kind of nodded your head. I wanted you to make some dazzling smile at me, but no such luck. You just flipped your hair back like a teenager and sipped your tea. I felt really nervous and looked over at the woman who was reading a book. She was still reading. Red sat down. I don't know how she did it with that big bustle on her. Then she lit a little cigar and offered me one. Of course I took it. "You two know each other long?" I asked.

Red winked. "Our whole lives."

"God, Nadine, I'm really glad to see you. I've missed you so much." Then I reached my hand out to touch you across the table. You looked me right in the eye. Then you picked up your tea cup, pushed your chair back, and walked out of the room.

I was sitting up in bed with Red who by now I called Esther. Both of us were naked. Her hair was down. She was smoking a cigar, and I was staring into the candlelight. She patted my cheek with her free hand. "You're a nice lover when you pay attention."

I took a drag off her cigar and looked at her. It was really nice sex, some of the nicest I've had in my lesbian life. It was hard to enjoy it, though, because I was mostly thinking about you, Nadine.

"Listen *neshomeleh*, I wouldn't worry about this Nadine Pagan if I were you. Do you understand it isn't personal how she runs from you? Her heart is full of sorrow. She got no idea how to let it out or let something better in. You can love her as much as you want to, but in my humble opinion—speaking strictly as your friend—it's going to be some time before she's able to love you back. In the meantime, there's plenty to do around here."

"Like what?" I asked, wondering if I'm going to have to make them breakfast or clean their house.

"There's the little problem of patching up the world."

I thought about this for a minute and sat quiet against the

head of Red Esther's bed. All of a sudden, I don't know if it was because I hadn't smoked pot for a while, or I was lonely for you, Nadine, or patching up the world seemed like a lost cause, or what, I felt sadder than I ever felt in my life. I felt so sad I started crying and just couldn't stop.

Chapter 19

A Continuing Saga

One I minute I lie in bed an invalid, some pretty woman spooning one warm soup or another into my mouth. A minute later I am on my hands and knees in the middle of corpse piles eating shit. The next thing I know I'm crawling on my belly like a worm through a sewer pipe, and then, right after, I'm playing my violin from the stage of a crowded concert hall, not alone either, but with a whole orchestra of women. I find myself kneeling among nuns during evening prayers. Even stranger than that, one morning I stand with my sleeves rolled up discussing the fingering of a particularly difficult chord with my hero, Nicolo Paganini.

You may call this dreaming, Jane, but it is not, because if it were dreaming I would be awake by now. In spite of the swiftness with which I travel from minute to minute and time to time, there are some regular events in my life: breakfast on the beach and dinner in the kitchen with my new friends—Esther, Magda, Etta, and Shula. Long nights in a feather bed naked and alone or with red-headed Esther, or even Rose who has somehow managed to find me. Rose is alright to be close to here. She talks to me in a calmer way than she did in New Chelm, but still I cannot let her all the way into my heart. More precious than the pleasure of my naked body beside another woman's is the pleasure I take in speaking long sentences with remarkable ease, arguments by the fire with

Etta and Shula about *ideas*, complicated disagreements about the concepts of respect, love, power, and passion, and the ethical meanings of each. Rose wants to know all the time if I love her, but I am not sure yet what love means.

The other women here listen to me, care for me, carry me from place to place when I am too weak to travel alone, leave me in quiet when this is what I crave. Two nights ago Esther held a framed glass up to me. The woman I saw there was so beautiful, she made me cry. When I cried the woman in the glass cried too. Then Esther started laughing her head off, then I did, then the woman in the glass did too. I pointed.

"It's you, silly," Esther said, "that's you."

But she had no scar. The woman's face was clear and open. I touched my own face. No ridges around it. How could this be? Esther took me in her arms and danced me around the room. "It's those fancy arguments you're having with Shula and Etta," she whispered in my ear. "They're opening your face like a window." Then she kissed me and took me to bed.

Sometimes I do dream. I am running through the woods terrified. Dogs bark. My head is on fire. Three men stand in my path. Two more close in on either side. I try to call for help, but only teeth come out of my head. My head burns hotter. The men close in tighter. The dogs bark louder. I wake myself up screaming.

A beautiful wedding. You and Electa stand together, sisters under the *chuppa*. Our mother is the rabbi. All are dressed in white High Holy Day robes, even me. I am on the corner of the *bima*, my bow perched just above the strings of *Zaideh* Yitzhach's violin, ready for action. Mommy wears a diamond-shaped hat like they do on *Yom Kippur*. She spreads her long, beautiful hands up over your bowed heads, then nods at me to begin. I run my bow across the violin, and a chord rich and full as silk comes through me, rises from the *bima* into the synagogue, up, up into the heavens. I touch the strings gently and one by one, sweet, tender notes fill the space around me. Here at last is my prayer to you, Jane, to Electa, to even our mother. Here at last is the beauty of all I can give. The congregation, full of women, is rapt and attentive. Each note sings out, take my gift for your pleasure, my gratitude, my love. Mommy opens her hands, which sparkle in the light of stained-glass windows, she opens her hands and looks to me with a warm and cheery face. One more chord, thick and delicious. I draw my bow, the music wells up from my heart. Then, with an enormous crash that drowns out my crescendo, our father Mel tumbles out of the Holy Ark. He brushes himself off, embarrassed, then points his finger at me. I look at our mother who smiles at me gently until her teeth turn into fangs which glint in the light of the eternal flame.

This is no dream. I crawl on my belly through a sewer pipe. Electa and you are with me, Jane, and some others, men I do not know and have never seen. I have a gun stuck into the waistband of my skirt and am leading the way. I climb up rusty rungs and push a manhole cover out of the way. One by one we crawl on our bellies through the streets of Warsaw. A bullet whizzes over the tops of our heads, then another, then another. You pull the pin out of a hand grenade and toss it. I catch it with both my hands, then remember this hand grenade is not for me. I throw it full force into the night.

I sit in a tiny room facing Rose. I hold *Zaideh* Yitzhach's violin up to my chin, Rose holds a recorder to her lips, pursed, ready for action. She nods her head and we begin, a short duet so pleasant to the ear and heart it makes me giddy. Rose raises her eyebrows. "Again?" she asks. I nod this time and we play into the night.

"I love you so much, Nadine," I think Rose tells me, but really I am not certain this is what she said.

Breakfast by the sea again. Rose is staring into her glass of tea which Esther has taught her to drink with jelly or else with a sugar cube pressed under her tongue so that the warmth of the tea melts it slowly on contact.

It occurs to me that Rose is sad.

She reaches her hand out to me and I just barely touch it. I want to thank her for being here. I want to offer her another night in my bed, to honor her in some way for her bravery in the face of my resistance, to thank her for our little duet. Our eyes meet, and for a second I feel her touching my heart. I try to tell her I like her but my voice becomes gravel. My teeth feel glued together by wads of bubble gum. Esther taps Rose on the shoulder and leads her into the house. "Good-bye, Nadine," Rose tells me, and I almost feel sad.

Chapter 20

Evidence To The Contrary

Kria stuck by me through the winter, and for this I am grateful. Without her I would have walled myself up in my little apartment, burned *yortseit* candles, studied, and starved. She brought me soup, wrapped me in my winter coat, and took me to movies, even forced me to come to some of her political meetings. I found her in my bed more nights than not, and little by little I came back to life.

After a while the sewer dream returned once a month rather than once a week. Its meaning finally was clear: Nadine, Electa, and I were rats running through our family shit. We were ill-clad, but we had some ammunition. It was our job to save each other, although we weren't allowed to open our mouths to do it. It was as simple as that.

Spring arrived full-blown, exactly on schedule in the middle of March. One really warm morning, Kria came and found me in the lab, dragged me outside, and put me on her motorcycle. "This is to make up for all those love dates we missed last summer," she told me. She started the engine and off we rode into the woods past the campus, up into the hills that pass as mountains in the Chelm Valley.

It was hard to do, but with every twist of the road, every curve swinging further away from school, past farmhouses, along stone walls, my heart became lighter. Biological facts flew out of my brain, and with them all the nightmares of winter. I was flying, my arms clinging to the waist of a woman who loved me, unequivocally, in spite of my family, my loyalties.

We rode for maybe an hour until Kria cut up onto a gravel road, coaxed the bike gently along a muddy path, then stopped on the edge of an open field. Most of the snow was melted, but you could still smell winter escaping from the ground.

"Whose place is this?"

Kria hopped down from the bike and snapped off her helmet. "Woman in town named Willa Kaufman. This is kind of a community playground. Come on."

She took my hand and started running up a trail that led to another trail and another, steadily climbing until we were deep in the woods standing on beautiful rock cliffs. "Me and a bunch of other dykes helped build that cabin over there." She gestured toward a small house that poked up out of the trees. "More like a shack, really. We worked our asses off for two months a few summers ago, so it felt like a cabin then." Kria had her arm around me and herded me to the house. The ground was a little soggy and rocky, but the air was wonderful. I felt like I was breathing for the first time since Electa announced her engagement.

"Looks like somebody broke in." Kria inspected the broken padlock on the flimsy door. She opened it gingerly and poked her head in. "Someone was here alright, but everything looks OK—they just slept here or something." I followed her in. She leaned over and sniffed the mattress. "I don't think it was guys. Once in a while dykes who don't know Willa come up and use the land. The ones who don't believe in private property like to break in as a political statement." She went back out and fingered the hasp. "I'll fix it next time I'm here. Whoever it was broke in some time ago. I don't think there's anything to worry about now."

Kria came in again and closed the door behind her. She spread a red blanket out over the cot, unzipped her jacket, and draped it over a chair. I was terrified. But she pulled me to her with her fine strong arms and began to kiss me so attentively and so sincerely, I nearly came on the spot.

We made love for hours. It was the best sex I ever had. It was brave sex, I was an adult with another adult, and no members of my family were around to contest that fact. Even though Kria had been my lover for over a year, I had never enjoyed her like this. It was like starting over for me, and I felt fearless. We dozed, we woke, we covered each other everywhere with kisses, drove our fingers into every crevice and opening, yowled, wept, and finally became hysterical laughing. Then the light started to change. It got cold in the shack, and soon Kria's leather jacket wasn't enough to warm my naked body. I had to get dressed.

"When we get back down to town, I'm going to take you out for the best Chinese food you ever had in your life," she told me.

"That's great," I said, "but don't you think we should take advantage of our surroundings and hike around? I haven't been in the woods for about three years. I'd like to remember what it feels like while I'm scrubbing those test tubes tomorrow."

Kria looked at her watch. "We've got at least an hour before it gets dark. Come on—I'll take you down to the stream."

It was a good thing Kria was with me or I might have set my own head on fire. We were the picture of perfect academic lesbian love as we fairly skipped over rocks and fallen logs and one or two piles of unmelted snow. You could hear the water burbling just ahead through the trees. When we got to the bank, I pulled her close and buried my face deep into her neck, kissed her, held her. Then I opened my eyes and saw them.

Just the shoes at first, the worn-out round toes of somebody's work boots pointing toward the water. "What do you think that is?" I let go of Kria's arm and picked my way over to where the boots stood. That was when I saw the violin.

I didn't recognize it immediately. My first horrible thought was that it was some bony baby corpse left out as a sacrificial offering. When I got right up to it I saw that it was worse. The case was water-logged and swollen. The latches were rusted, but

157

when I pushed on them one at a time after working them a little, they sprung open. The velvet lining was mildewed and damp, and there, inside, was *Zaideh* Yitzhach's violin.

It was wrapped in a piece of silk that smelled like Nadine did when she jumped me in my car after the wedding. I uncovered the violin and inspected it for injuries. It was all in one piece, the finish even looked decent, but I had no idea if lying in the snow all winter had killed it, if anyone would ever be able to get a tune from it again.

I was panic-struck. The shoes pointed to the stream which certainly looked deep enough to drown in. The violin lay beside the shoes. If this was Nadine's violin, and those were her shoes, then where was my sister Nadine?

I got down on my knees and searched the river bank frantically for more signs of Nadine, for Nadine herself. Kria kept trying to hold me, to stop me, but I pushed her away. Every downed limb and exposed root was a truncated arm or leg, every jutting rock a severed hand or foot. I scrambled from false trace to false trace on all fours like a bloodhound. I saw my face in the stream and dove in.

The water was freezing, colder than anything I could remember. Kria paced on the shore, pleading with me to come out. But I was determined. I dove, swam, dove again, until at last at the bottom of the river I began to find pieces of Nadine: one sock a flannel shirt a torn pair of jeans. One by one I handed these up to Kria, who by now was sitting on a log shaking her head. When I handed up the vest Kria took it and then held tight to my hand.

"You've gotta get out of there, you'll freeze to death."

She helped me out and I stood shivering over the soggy pile of what used to be my sister. Kria took her jacket off and wrapped it around me. "Jesus Christ," she said, "where the hell is her body?" Kria put her jacket over my shoulders. It was getting dark and I was freezing, but I wasn't ready to give up yet.

"Walk with me for a little way along the bank. I promise, if we don't find any more in a half hour I'll quit."

Half a mile down, a mass of fallen trees and branches made a tangled dam across the stream. All kinds of debris gathered there—including a notebook and a pair of cotton underpants—but no body, no Nadine. I climbed into the water and retrieved the notebook. The pages were washed out and nearly erased, but there were enough marks remaining for me to clearly see musical notes on some of the pages. Kria took the notebook from me and put it on top of the rest of Nadine's wet things. I scooped up the violin and shoes and together, in the nearly dark, we trudged down through the woods to Kria's bike. Kria pushed all the soft things down into one of her saddle bags, then tied the shoes to the back fender. I held the violin between us and held on to her as tightly as I could. It is a miracle to me that the whole long way back to New Chelm, although it occurred to me more than once, I never let go of Kria, never leaned or leaped or tumbled off the bike, did not simply let go and fall backwards into the cool air and darkness that threatened to swallow me up.

Chapter 21

A Message From The Dead

Ho Jane, ho ho Jane, despair not. I am alive and well and living with our sisters. Not Electa, not you Jane, the other sisters, the Jewish nuns and the Jewish witches, the Jewish dead and the Jewish alive. Ho Jane, I am down here with the survivors, with the girl scouts and the kapos, the whores and the suffragettes. I am down here with the wimmin who fought back when their daddies finger-fucked them in their cradles and the womyn who traced their ways through underground tunnels to get a people out of the ghettos. Ho Jane, here I am standing on the sidewalk while dozens of women dive out of the Triangle Shirtwaist Factory. Ho Jane, watch me now in a parachute dive out of a plane behind enemy lines and live to tell about it but not for long. Ho Jane, over here Jane, there's a million teen-age girls who set their heads on fire, slit their wrists, married a doctor, and also became a doctor, went to law school, won a Pulitzer prize for poetry, went on to be pushy big mouths ho Jane, ho ho Jane, I'm not dead, I'm more alive than you are. Don't worry. I will rise up from the dead place and join you like a plant from the ground like moss like sea weed, I am coming back, ho Jane, to repent and join you. Ho Jane, do not despair. I will be loving you soon.

Chapter 22

They Came From Underground

Nadine, all I can say is, it was a good thing that those women through the mirror taught me as much as they did, or by the time I came back to New Chelm and the land of our day-to-day lives, I would have been one sorry, heartbroken case. How many times did I try to touch you and you turned away? I made myself play musical instruments I knew nothing about just to be close to you, but even that didn't open your heart. Maybe it did. Sometimes I could kind of see a glimmer of love in your faraway eyes, but most of the time you were gone.

That's why I'm so glad for all the hard work Etta and Shula forced me to do. They sure got my mind more or less off of you and onto the big business at hand. I mean, who would have thought that I, Rose Shapiro, would ever in my life find myself actually participating in fabulous acts of resistance and learning. You know me, Nadine, up until then my idea of being radical was smoking a joint on the New Chelm town commons.

This was a new life, one filled with meaning and a strong sense of purpose. Like that unbelievable meat riot when all us women broke windows up and down the Lower East side of Manhattan because our children were starving. I was just kind of standing there at first in a doorway, you know. I didn't know what to think about anything or what to do. Then this young woman came up to me all smashed up in her face and says, "Missus, can you help me?" I pretended like I didn't understand her at first. I didn't want to get involved. I was just into watching. Then all of a sudden Etta comes up beside me and says, "Of course we'll help you." and we bring this woman up to some kitchen. Etta sits her down and says, "So Rose, help me clean her up." I just stood there. I couldn't move until Etta points to the hallway and says, "Run, get water, quick." Which I did.

That marked the beginning of my understanding of the true nature of work. That it wasn't just about chopping up vegetables with my head in a dopey fog and throwing them into a pot to make soup. It meant bigger things, like running guns and food, false papers and real messages behind all kinds of enemy lines. It wasn't fun, it was shit-in-your-pants terrifying, but it showed me that there was a lot more to life than my romantic problems. It also did a great deal for my self-esteem. There were times when we would be running for our lives—Esther, Etta, Shula, and me—I mean running like crazy, and someone would ask me, "Rose, take this bundle into the trenches," and I would say, "What, are you crazy? I don't do that kind of stuff." Then the next thing I know I'm running down an alley with a sack full of hand grenades without thinking anything about it. Because why? It was my job.

I learned how to work very hard on the other side of the mirror and I loved it, I really did, but finally I realized it was time to go back to New Chelm. It never got easier to be around you when you didn't want me, Nadine. The women on the other side of the mirror were good women, but they weren't my women. There was no *Lechem V'Shalom*, no Crystal, no baggy-pants-flannel-shirt girls to drive me crazy. I was kind of lonesome for all those women over at the restaurant, and I was lonely to talk to women who really knew me. About real stuff. I wanted to show the New Chelm women what I'd learned about how to have community. I wanted to ask them how I was supposed to want to be a responsible lesbian citizen if no one bothered to talk to me, if they just kicked me out of my room and made up stuff about me behind my back?

I would miss you, Nadine, but it was clear from all my attempts and failed attempts at hugging, kissing, or otherwise making out with you that we weren't getting anywhere with each other. Even people who only knew you for a couple of lifetimes like Red Esther said the same thing: Nadine Pagan and intimacy weren't going to be words in the same sentence for a long time. Just because I got to sleep with you once in a while, or even make music all night with you on an instrument I had no idea I knew how to play, didn't mean we were going to get any closer. I was sad about that but I didn't feel hopeless, which for me was a refreshing change of pace.

Right before I left you the most amazing thing happened. It was that really, really big wedding where about a hundred people were marrying each other, and we all were women. It was the coolest thing I ever saw. There were tons of us, dressed up in fancy clothes. We were in this enormous synagogue, like so big I couldn't believe it. It was like a convention hall, only this building was about a couple of hundred years old. There were wooden pews to sit on with fancy velvet covers, and there was a balcony but no women had to go sit in it. We were all downstairs, and Red was the rabbi for a while and then Etta was and then Magda and Shula, they all took turns. There was this beautiful silk canopy full of flowers called a *chuppa* that four women held up. Those women wore white shirts, white pants, no shoes. All us brides danced in down the aisle. We were the most beautiful women I ever saw in my life if I do say so myself.

We crowded the main floor of this synagogue dancing with each other. Some of us had that spectacular shining black Jewish hair that curls and frizzes and flies in every direction, and some had blonde hair that hung around their heads like halos. Some had tight curly close-to-the-head hair, and some had beautiful scarves of many colors tied around their heads with fabulous earrings dangling down against their slender necks and I couldn't tell if they had any hair at all. There were brides in flowing robes, brides in jeans and turtlenecks, brides in bustles, brides in dashikis. Some had bare feet, some fancy shoes, some had work boots or high-tops. Everyone was dancing. Under the *chuppa* and through the synagogue, hand in hand in hand. And what music! Tubas and tambourines, clarinets, trombones. And at the very center of all of this, high on the shoulders of the brides themselves, you were carried, my beloved Nadine. You, Nadine, who would marry none of us and all of us this night. We would carry you high above our heads like the *Torahs* on the one Jewish holiday I can remember, *Simchat Torah*, that holiday on which the *Torahs*, having been read from one scroll to the other, are danced about and celebrated as if they are God themselves. On this night we were all of us *Torahs*, dancing and praying and kissing and marrying. We were drunk on each other, so beautiful each one.

It became, as if by magic, quiet in the synagogue, reverential. All of us brides held hands with each other in a great spiral that filled the synagogue. We stood silently. Then, Nadine, you stood alone under the *chuppa*, that canopy of silk and roses, and played for us a song so ancient and beautiful that every woman in the room recognized it as her own. And so we wept and were joined in this way one to the other, each to each, and finally to you, Nadine, and I knew for certain that you would never be mine alone. And when you were done with your beautiful song, which was a classic Jewish mix of joy and sorrow, Red Esther let go of our hands and stood beside you under the *chuppa*. She held a beautiful glass goblet up to all of us and wrapped it in a linen handkerchief. This she put on the floor in front of you, Nadine, and you stomped on it with both feet. When it shattered we cheered, because it meant a prosperous union between us all. Then we lifted you again onto our shoulders and danced you around the synagogue and through the streets, where everyone ate and danced for what seemed like a week. We slept in tents when we felt like sleeping. It reminded me of the Michigan Womyn's Music Festival, only the food was a lot better. I mean there was every possible food—stuffed cabbages and figs, spiced dates mixed with nuts and honey, huge loaves of beautiful braided *challah*, gigantic circles of pita. There were soups and stews, carob and apples, oranges, almonds, felafals and rice. And because there was plenty, all were full.

One strange thing for me about this whole big party was that I completely forgot about getting high. Do you get it? Me, Rose Shapiro, at a party where I didn't give a flying fuck one way or the other if I got loaded or not? This was history. I just danced these dances I never knew I knew, and kissed all my sister brides. Once in a while I went off to someone's tent and we made love, but that was the other kind of funny thing. I was having such a good time at the party, I didn't want to miss anything, even to have good sex with some beautiful woman. *All* those women were really beautiful to me, and dancing and eating and telling jokes with them was really as much fun as having sex, and a lot less scary. The other really weird thing was, sometimes I caught sight of you, Nadine, and it made me sad and distracted for a few minutes, but after a while it didn't bother me at all.

Little by little people started packing up and going home, and I knew it was time now for me to go back to New Chelm. Every woman was kissing every other one sweetly, or with an awe-inspiring passion, or some combination of both. I was ready to pack up my things and head back. I was reluctant to go because part of me wanted to be in a place where I could look upon you forever, Nadine, and love you that way. But then Red and Magda came and found me while I was making sure all my magic was in order in my knapsack. Red was in her blue satin bathrobe, and her hair was down, and I must admit it was hard to keep my mind on packing. All of a sudden we weren't on the street any more. We were at the kitchen table and Magda was pouring coffee into demitasse cups.

"You look like you're planning on heading up," Magda said. She held a sugar cube in a pair of tongs over my cup. I nodded and the cube plopped loudly into the coffee.

"I think it's for the best," Red said. She lit a cigar and offered me one. I declined. I sipped my coffee which was so strong it made me wince. I wanted to know if you would be coming to say good-bye to me, Nadine, but I was too nervous to ask out loud.

Esther knocked back the last of her coffee and held her cup out to Magda for more. "Don't worry about Nadine for now. You'll have another chance with her, I'm certain. Finish your coffee and say good-bye to Magda. I'll take you to the starting-off place myself."

We walked, rowed, swam and walked again until we came to the same stone cliff, the same little cave of light I had seen so often in my dreams. Red Esther put her arms around me and held me close.

"We'll meet again," she told me. "The way you're going is right through there." She pointed to the cave where I swear to God, Nadine, someone who looked just like me was standing naked beckoning me toward her. I turned to kiss Red Esther good-bye, but she was gone. There was nowhere to go but toward myself.

It was like an elevator ride through an ice box. I was flying through time and space again. I recognized the languages around me now as Yiddish and Ladino, which was not so strange, since actually a lot of people I was just visiting talked in those exact languages and I talked back in them too. There were strains of music all around me, and *whoosh whoosh*, it seemed to take forever and it wasn't even fun. My heart was broken and full at the same time. Before I knew it, I was home.

I stepped out of my mirror. It was night, although what night I didn't know. I lay on the floor exhausted and soon was fast asleep.

I woke up with a start in front of the bedroom closet. I don't know how long I lay there running over where I just was in my head like some mammoth dream. Only I was pretty sure it wasn't a dream, all those women dancing and my days and nights with you and Red Esther. I sat up and felt around my pockets, but I found no tangible proof of where I had been. Then I poked my head out the window. The sky was really blue, and the snow was all melted. That didn't mean anything. Around this part of Massachusetts winter sometimes disappeared overnight.

My apartment was very dusty. Under the couch it was a real gross-a-rama, but that didn't tell me anything either. I went down to my mailbox. Two phone bills, three gas bills (along with an if-you-don't-pay-within-ten-days-you're-fucked notice), and a note from the true tenant of the apartment wondering how things were going, oh, and incidentally she would be coming back to New Chelm on April first, could I be out by then. There was also a note from Crystal:

> *Rose, where the hell are you? I have been here three times so far, you're not in your apartment. If you don't show up to work by Friday, that's it you're out. For the collective, Crystal.*

I went back upstairs and tried the stove. The gas was still on so I wasn't gone *that* long. Then I got pissed off. I called the restaurant. Someone I didn't know answered. "Is Crystal there?" There was a pause and then Crystal got on the line. "This is Rose," I said.

"Jesus Christ, Rose, where the hell have you been? On some month-long bender or something?"

"Month-long bender? Me?"

"Oh yeah, right, you're on a life-long bender."

That was a slap in the face I wasn't expecting. I didn't say yeah, fuck you, but I thought about it. "I haven't been gone that long."

"Missing work for six weeks without calling in is a pretty long time. Nobody knew where you were. We got one of your neighbors to check your apartment out because we got scared. Your car was there, you weren't dead or anything, we just figured you went out of town—"

"You didn't call the cops did you?"

"With all that shit in your apartment why would we call the cops? We're pissed, not stupid. Where were you?"

"Away."

Crystal let out an exasperated sigh. "I've got to get to work on the lunch prep. You probably figured you're out of a job—"

I didn't say anything.

"If you want to discuss that, we're open to it, but honestly Rose, you were totally irresponsible and this time I couldn't cover for you."

I hung up the phone and stared at the mirror. I pushed my fingers on the glass. Nothing budged. I pushed again and again. Still nothing.

I went into the bathroom and pushed the mirror there. Solid glass. Maybe this was one gigantic hallucination, in which case all those dykes in the rooming house and at *Lechem V'Shalom* were right. Marijuana was ruining my brain.

I filled the bathtub and peeled my shirt off. It sure smelled like I was wearing it for weeks. Then I pulled off my shoes which were muddy, and sure enough, right in the middle of my left shoe, squashed flatter than a pancake, was that joint I rolled just in case I was going to need it. Now I had to ask myself two questions. Number one, why would I smoke dope for six weeks and pass out and then wake up in my clothes right in front of the bedroom closet, and number two, why would I do it with a joint in my shoe? Did I hit the closet door and then knock myself out? Was I passed out for six weeks, or does time go in a different direction on the other side of the mirror? No wonder I was exhausted. But here is the strangest part of everything. I climbed into the bathtub, I lit a candle, I closed my eyes, and then I climbed out and went to bed. Nowhere from the tub to my bed, or even when I got up a few hours later to walk around in the world, did it ever occur to me to smoke a joint. I stared at the squashed joint, I looked at the pot hanging like clothes in my closet, and I was honestly baffled. What was it doing there? Why did I have it?

I walked down to town and got a cup of coffee. Then I noodled back around through the woods up to my house. It was spring. I was full of something new that was budding inside me. It was hard to look at parts of New Chelm and not be wondering always where were you now, Nadine, what were you doing? Were you with Red Esther, or Magda, or fighting some war? I had the picture firmly in my head whether I was actually with you or not.

I came back to the apartment and examined what was left of my summer dope stock. There wasn't a lot of it, but there was enough to beckon me with its sweet smell. All of a sudden I didn't care what it smelled like. I didn't want it in my closet anymore. I gathered it up in plastic trash bags and stuffed it into the trunk of my car. I was out of a job. I was out of a place to live. I had no lover. I had about three hundred dollars worth of pot which I could sell if I wanted, but I didn't want to. In a couple of days I would bring it all back to where it came from. I would return the pot to Willa Kaufman's land.

Part 4

Chapter 23

A Great Return

The big wedding is over and they carry me down to the river, my sisters, not you Jane, nor even Electa, my new sisters Esther and Etta, Magda and Shula, and with them all of the women, dozens more. I am on a stretcher made of rushes woven together, and they carry me down and down to the river and wash me in perfumes and oils. Each woman touches my face and my heart. They are naked here by the fire, and me I am naked too. They tell me things in a secret language, each one whispering her own good-bye, each one telling her love to me and also her sorrow.

One by one and all together they sing to me great, sad songs, and finally Etta and Esther, Shula and Magda, lift the rushes with me on them up on their shoulders and carry me, lay me down in the water, cover me with petals from many flowers, bid me farewell. I wave from my raft of rushes, a thin arm rising as the river carries me away.

"We'll see you again," they tell me, but in minutes I am alone.

The raft carries me so swiftly that all the sky is a great blur until I am all of me under water. The little raft flies out from under me, the petals float everywhere around me, and I am swimming back, back to my sad point of origin, full and empty all in one.

At last I begin my climb up through the waters. Naked I brush past branches and leaves, tumble toward sunlight, spin, float, become leaden, until finally I splash up into the chilly air and drag myself onto the river bank.

Where are my clothes? I threw them into this river, none have washed up. But where are my shoes? Where is our *Zaideh* Yitzhach's violin? Those I know I left by some rock or other not far from here and yet I don't see them. Like a dog I dig. Who has them I wonder and wonder. Who has my shoes? Ho Jane, ho Jane, is it you is it you?

The ground under my feet is muddy and cold. There are still some snow piles on the path, and even melting they come up to my knees. Naked I shiver to the cabin and push open the door. I tug the red blanket off the bed and wrap it around me. I tie pillowcases around my feet and sit on the empty cot. What should I do? What am I to do? I touch a finger to my cheek. My scar has returned.

I can think of only one thing. I must find my violin. I go back to the river and turn over rocks, pull out trees. My blanket and pillowcase feet are covered with mud, but I can't find our *Zaideh* Yitzhach's violin anywhere, not a trace of it, not a string or a piece of horse hair. Where is my violin?

Suddenly I am exhausted and starving. Suddenly I remember everything. Electa's wedding, all the other weddings. I remember setting my hair on fire and living in the hospital. I remember times in bed with Rose I could not tolerate and other times I did. I remember standing in shit with Magda, lying in bed with Esther, eating with a dozen women all at the same time. I remember jumping naked into the water and why did I leave my violin behind it was everything to me and now it is gone. Is anything better now than it was before?

I am exhausted and starving and I must go home. To you, Jane, to Electa and Mommy. I am new now and ready to forgive you, to embrace you, to be forgiven. I gather the muddy blanket around me and trudge down the hill to the main road, just as a strange spring snow begins to fall.

◊ ◊ ◊

Snowflakes cover my eyelashes, fill my hair. I think, at last I am freezing to death. I think also of our ancestors who have walked in this way before me, their feet wrapped in rags, or like my boy-self who traveled the forests of Poland, Germany, France. From Vilna to Grodno, from Grodno to Minsk, from Minsk to Moscow, to Siberia and back. I made this journey not long ago as a little boy, but all that is a dream to me now, I can't piece it together in any order. I only wish that those sweetest women would come and find me. Now is when I need them, on my way to our family and with no violin to comfort me. Where is that sweet wine and honey cake?

I try to imagine: a warm summer day, leaves shady and green, birds singing sweetly in the tree tops. But my feet are freezing. How did we do it? Me and those great-great-grandparents of ours? I hear strains of violin music, a tune our grandmother taught me so many years before, not the *frailech* that turned our mother against me forever, but a lullaby, sweet, embracing. I hum it in my head. It makes me sleepy.

I have made it to the main road and here I sit down, for it is a road no longer but instead a bed of warm white down. Little men with sidelocks and beards, broad-brimmed hats and gabardines, dance around me. Around those men dance Etta, Magda, Shula, Esther, Rose, and even you, Jane, you dance too. Sometimes you are all of you naked and sometimes dressed, sometimes everyone turns old, and other times everyone is someone I never met. I try to join you in your spinning but I cannot move. The snow on my eyelashes weighs me down. The music is soft and far away.

I lay my head down in the soft sweet snow and find what I crave here—deep, delicious sleep.

Chapter 24

Rescue

My meeting with those *Lechem V'Shalom* dykes was worse than I expected. I mean, it wouldn't have mattered if I brought in a sworn affidavit from my family psychiatrist saying I'd never smoke dope again. Everyone was into this thing like, what was to say I wasn't going to just up and disappear for two months again some other time and frankly they were sick of it and this was a feminist collective for God's sake and what the hell was my problem that I thought I could just do whatever I goddamn wanted to and then come marching right back into a job that there were lesbians ready to kill for? Then this one weasel dyke who happened to be the driving force behind getting me kicked out of the rooming house, and who already had my job at the restaurant, got into this whole thing about how did they know I wasn't going to sell pot at the restaurant? Boy, I wanted to slug her. She made me so mad I wanted to light up right there. Of course I didn't because all my dope was out in the car and I hadn't had any—well, maybe a toke or two—since I got back from visiting you in mirror city.

It did occur to me to tell them where I had gone. I mean, there were enough of those magical lesbian types around that I could actually say, "You think you're Queen Tut from Planet Lesbo? Well, the real reason I've been gone for six weeks is that I fell into a mirror and ended up living all my past lives simultaneously."

But the fact was, since I came back I couldn't even stick a fingertip through any mirrors in my house, never mind my whole body. Maybe I did make the whole thing up. Only my dreams kept me remembering that there was a place where you were alive, Nadine. It came with a house full of women with Jewish names who liked me just fine the way I was, and there was always something useful I could do there, always some important work. Mostly I was just sad that I couldn't figure out how to go back. But I knew it now. I knew I had something to look forward to and behind at. So when those dykes started yelling at me one more time, when that weasel dyke told me it was outrageous that I would even consider coming back to work at *Lechem V'Shalom* and even Crystal agreed, I looked at them all and said, "Fine." I walked out of the restaurant and went straight to my car.

Because that was the other thing. I had nowhere else to go. The original renter of my apartment was back in town. She showed up at my door with her matching luggage and her matching girlfriend at 6:00 A.M. on April first and gave me one of those fake-warm rich lesbian hugs. She introduced me to her girlfriend. "Didn't you get my note?" she asked.

"Gosh no," I lied.

She kind of sashayed into the apartment and sat down at the kitchen table with her lover. They took up both chairs. "You don't have any coffee do you? Oh, Rose, I can't believe you didn't get my letter. What a drag." I may have been wrong but I think she was pouting. Her matching girlfriend pouted too.

They both looked up at me expectantly while I stood there like a big dope in my bathrobe. I think they were waiting for me to take their order.

The good thing about girls with money is they can take a change in plans better than many of the rest of us. After a cup of coffee, a lot of sighing, and a few disparaging remarks about the U.S. postal system, she made some phone calls, stared at me kind of serious, and said, "We'll stay with friends of mine over near the university for a couple of weeks. I'm sorry it's such short notice, Rose, but you really have to be out by the fifteenth. OK?"

Well, here it was the fifteenth. I had no place to live, no job, and no possibility of getting either one back. What was the point of trying to go back to Vick Street? That weasel lesbian probably had my old room by now anyway.

All my shit was stuffed in the trunk and back seat of my car. If I really wanted to, I could go out to Verna and Leslie's in Boston, which didn't seem like such a bad idea. I made a couple of long-distance phone calls while I was in my last weeks at the plush apartment, and Verna told me that on the fifteenth she and Leslie were taking off for Vermont to spend Passover with her sister. I could stay in their apartment until they got back and then maybe we could work something out long-term. I loved Verna. She really got it about shared space and broken hearts.

So after this long stupid meeting with the *Lechem V'Shalom* collective that's what I did. I got right into my car and drove to Verna and Leslie's the back way, which would take me up past the land so I could say good-bye to my favorite place in the world on the way to Boston. I would toss all that beautiful pot back where it came from and then I would start my life again with old friends who understood me and weren't going to give me a lot of shit for fucking up.

Who cared if I was so pissed off I wanted to burn and destroy every lesbian collectively run anything in the entire town of New Chelm? I was a free woman now with my whole life ahead of me. I was on my way to Boston on the most beautiful road I knew. Then what do you think happened?

It started to snow. Not just normal itty-bitty spring snow. Out of nowhere, I am in the middle of a fucking blizzard. *Oh, this is rich*, I thought. *Here I am two weeks into April, a refugee from my lesbian home trying to find peace and solace in a new place, and what do I do? I drive smack into some record-breaking Northeaster that should have been a hurricane.*

I controlled myself and slowed down. I had absolutely no idea where I was and only a slightly better one about where I might be

181

going. I skidded and pulled, spun my wheels and chugged forward, when all of a sudden I saw this snow-covered thing trundling down the middle of the road. *Great,* I thought, *driven to exile by a failed lesbian community, our heroine comes upon an abominable snow person and is devoured before she can begin a new life.*

I stopped the car and for a minute just sat and watched this thing come toward me. It occurred to me then that it wasn't a thing, it was a person wrapped in a red robe or something with pillowcases on its feet. Whatever it was it was coming right at me. Without warning it just stopped and boom, sat down. I couldn't help myself. I had to get out of the car and see what was going on.

It took me a minute to make it over the ice, but when I finally saw who it was I couldn't believe it. There, frosted over like a life-sized lesbian paperweight, was you, my truest love, Nadine Pagan, sitting naked, except for Willa Kaufman's red blanket, smack in the middle of the road.

I gathered you up in my arms and carefully sat you down in the front seat of my car. I turned up the heat and untied those pillowcase shoes you had around your feet. I held your icy toes in my hands. You weren't out cold or anything but you could barely open your eyes. You squinted and looked at me as best you could, then you tried to say something which I think was supposed to be my name.

I looked up from your feet, Nadine, and touched your face. "Don't say anything, baby, it's OK. Just nod for me, can you feel this?" I squeezed your toes. You nodded. "I don't think you have frostbite, we'll have to get you inside real quick." Which, and I didn't say this to you, was going to be somewhat of a problem since neither of us had any place to live.

You looked into my eyes, Nadine, and I was a goner. "Hey, Nadine, the last time I saw you you were all dressed up. What happened to your fancy clothes?" I pulled my own jacket off and wrapped it around you. Then I took a pair of socks out from my trunk and put them on your feet. "You're frozen, honey, but you'll be OK I'll get you somewhere and take care of you."

I touched the scar around your face and then remembered the last time I saw you it wasn't there. I didn't know where to go or what to do. I thought, shit, I'll take you up to the cabin and drove the rest of the way in silence. I held onto your hand the whole time.

I maneuvered the car through the snow as far as I could and parked. I filled my knapsack with some more socks and a couple pairs of pants and a flannel shirt and lifted you in my arms. I carried you up the path to the cabin. It took forever, but we finally got there.

I kicked the door open and, without a word, lay you down on the cot. I started up a fire in the wood stove. I melted some snow and when the water was warm, I unwrapped you from your blanket and bathed you, then wrapped you in one of my flannel shirts and covered you with a dry blanket I found under the cot.

I looked at you, this disheveled Nadine, and could see you in a feather bed, or across from me at a kitchen table far away. But the fact was, you were here, Nadine Pagan, little and naked on the cot in Willa Kaufman's cabin, real as could be.

I sat on the floor and stared dumbly into space.

Chapter 25
Reunion

Here, Jane, I am brought to life.

Rose Shapiro lays me down on the skinny bed climbs in over me covers me with the whole of her body kisses me slowly on the forehead licks at my eyelids whispers into me I love you with her fingers traces the ring around my face tastes each of my purple ridges with her tongue presses her cheek flat against mine presses into me with the weight of her body embraces me breast to breast belly to belly knee to knee cunt to cunt lays against me until our breath comes together until I reach my frozen arms around Rose hold her breathe with her under her into her while Rose kisses my throat my neck my shoulders my cheeks my eyes my mouth which opens opens opens to Rose to Rose's tongue when our two tongues meet how we shudder together how we open and push and suck Rose pushes open my legs with her own rocks into me holds me whispers I love you we are here together now and a great cry comes up from me not a sex cry not a passion moan a cry of relief comes up from me and I pull Rose tighter my face covered with tears I try to speak but I cannot.

Rose puts her hand to my mouth I kiss the fingers wail into them shudder while Rose holds me you are home now and forgiven she says and a great sorrow cracks open inside me and is loosed at last upon the world.

◊ ◊ ◊

Through the snowy afternoon I sleep, wrapped in Rose's arms. I dream I am sitting at a huge *Pesach* table with our *Zaideh* Yitzhach, and you, Jane, Electa, and our mother Fay, also Rose and Esther, Etta, and Shula all of whom are pleased as punch and giggle like school girls as they put aside their *haggadahs*. I am a little boy again. I stand with a glass of wine in my hands and sing four questions in Hebrew. When I am finished, everyone applauds. Our Grandma Minnie comes out of the kitchen with an enormous platter of food. She leans over and kisses me on the cheek. "*Naches*, you give us, you sweet little *boychik*." The entire table agrees.

I wake up with a start and look around me. Still I am in bed with Rose. The same bed I lay in all those days and all those nights after Electa's wedding. Bit by bit I remember the women underwater my naked trek through strange country my rescue at the hands of Rose. I touch my face. It is still scarred. Outside snow falls in wild, fat flakes.

All at once I remember: My conviction to return to you all. To forgive and be forgiven. To ask for peace and to give peace within the family, our *mishpacha*. I will come back to you humbly, present myself respectfully, and play for you all that I have learned about loving and love.

And then I am panicked. I have lost *Zaideh* Yitzhach's violin. How can I show you how deep is my love without music to protect me? I breathe shallow like a puppy. Rose wakes up beside me, she puts an arm around me. She touches my face.

"I must go home, I must go home, but how can I go home without my violin?"

"Which home?" Rose asks me. She pulls a blanket around us. "I kind of like living here." She tries to kiss me, but I pull away.

"I must go home to my family. I have to tell them everything. I have to tell them everything, but now I've lost my violin."

Rose reaches out, puts both arms around me, draws me close in the bed. She smooths my hair. "You haven't been home for a long time, Nadine. You don't have to go now."

I shiver in Rose's arms. "I . . . must . . . go . . . home." Then I remember. "I have no clothes! I must find clothes and start walking now. They must forgive me and I must forgive them." I remember again, "I have lost my great-grandpa's violin."

Rose holds my hand and looks in my eyes. "There are three feet of snow out there. You can't walk to Worcester. You'll freeze."

"I must return. I must. I must."

"You can't walk all the way in the middle of a snowstorm—"

"I have no clothes."

"Even with clothes, you'll freeze." Rose kisses me and pulls on her pants. "If we can get the car out, I'll drive you to your family. I'll go with you even, inside their house."

"But I have no clothes."

"I've got a lot of clothes in the car," she tells me, and holds me in her arms until I am calm.

Chapter 26

The *Tsimmes* At *Pesach*

There was no body, only a shell of my sister: a few clothes, the remnants of some music she wrote, and the bones of her—our *Zaideh* Yitzhach's—violin. Kria and I told Willa Kaufman about our fears, and she was kind enough to act like a responsible lesbian citizen and ask the police to search her land. She had enough economic clout in the real world to ask them to do it respectfully and discreetly, and they did.

I was surprised she took us seriously, but Willa Kaufman understood that lesbians periodically traveled to secluded places and did themselves in or were done in by strangers. Two area police spent the better part of an afternoon on the land and combed it carefully. They found little more than I had. No missing fingers, no pieces of scalp, no teeth, no extraneous head, or loose toes. Only one thing that I had not found, a muddy sock. Given the romantic nature of the land, that could have belonged to anyone.

Did I tell my parents that I had evidence of Nadine or Nadine-no-longer? I did not. I kept the shoes and violin wrapped up in a blanket in my bedroom. I stared at them as if they were Nadine herself. I bought a *yortseit* candle and burned it. I wore a black armband and ripped my favorite shirt. I stopped going to classes. I sent Kria away. There was no body. No proof.

Only parts of my sister left neatly in a pile, parts I could not imagine she would leave behind willingly. Her shoes and her soul. She had to be dead; I couldn't make it fit together any other way. If I spoke to my parents, I'd have to tell them. I couldn't tell them because such news would kill them. Electa and I would be orphans. I was too old to be adopted and too young to accept a survivor's fate.

Then one day the phone rang and the ice cracked. My mother invited me to come home for Passover. "We haven't seen you since before *Hanukkah*. You'd think you lived in California. Electa and Mickey are coming in for the *seder*, and Mickey's parents."

"Do your old mom and dad a favor," my father chimed in from the other phone, "let us see your smiling face."

"Come in a little early and help me why don't you? It's the first time since the wedding that we'll all be together. I want it to be perfect."

My mother sounded hopeful. I stared at my *yortseit* candle. It flickered over Nadine's shoes and *Zaideh* Yitzhach's violin.

"Jane," my father was pleading, "it'll be just like old times."

Two weeks later, I packed a small backpack and the extant evidence of my sister Nadine into the trunk of my car. I had timed my drive so that I'd arrive at my parents' house a little after breakfast. That would give me enough time to tell my mother my theory about Nadine, that it wasn't just a metaphor anymore, she really was dead. True, my message would ruin tonight's *seder*, but I didn't care. I had to tell them everything or the burden of my knowledge would crush me. Besides, what better time to pass on horrible news. Electa was just an hour away and would take care of everything.

As I drove from New Chelm I rehearsed my delivery. Like a great lawyer, I would present Fay with the evidence. Here are Nadine's shoes. Here is her violin. My mother would wring her hands in sorrow, but at the same time heave a sigh of relief. She would call my father at work, he would come home immediately, and together they would call Electa in Boston. Electa would arrive with Mickey or without him. My secret would be shared, and finally I would be free. It was an excellent plan. We would mourn as a family and at last put my sister Nadine to rest. I played the scene over and over in my head as I passed pine trees and gas stations. Then, about twenty miles outside of Worcester, the weather got strange. It started to snow and snow.

By the time I made it up the hill to my parents' house and through their front door, half a foot of snow had fallen and I was an hour late. When I walked in the door my mother was frantically doing everything at once—polishing the silver, stuffing the chicken, stirring the soup. "Jane, I'm so glad you got here," she said, breathlessly pulling on her overshoes so she could shovel the sidewalk. "Cut up these potatoes and stick them in the pot around the chicken. Of all days to have a blizzard! I only hope Mickey and Electa can get here from Boston with Mickey's folks."

I took off my coat and shoes and began to act like a dutiful daughter. When my mother came in from shoveling, I would tell her everything. In the meantime I would do what I was asked. I was scrubbing potatoes and starting to peel them when the phone rang. It was my Aunt Miriam.

"When d'ya get in, Jane?"

"Just a few minutes ago."

"Good thing. It's a blizzard you know."

I looked out the window. It was still snowing like crazy.

"Is the *seder* still on?"

"I don't know, Aunt Miriam. My mother will call you,"

"Where is she?"

"She's out front shoveling the walk."

"Shoveling the walk? My God, I hope she doesn't have a heart attack!"

Just then the door flew open and my mother stood in the hall-way, stomping her feet and breathing heavily. "Honest to God, did you ever see anything like this?"

"Ma," I said, "Aunt Miriam is on the phone. Do you want to call her back?"

"Don't be silly!" My mother pulled her boots off and grabbed the phone.

I went back to my potatoes.

"Miriam, have you ever seen anything so crazy in your life? I just shoveled the walk and it's already covered up again. I hope the Robbins can make it . . . ."

I helped my mother by doing childhood chores. I polished silver, swept floors, dusted until the house glistened. I looked for a crack in my mother's incredible organization, a time to sit her down over a cup of tea and break the news. But whenever I tried to slow her down, to stop her, she'd put her hand up and say, "Please, Jane—I have so much to do."

At last it was lunchtime. Like a magician my mother covered the table with a minor feast including matzohs and *gefilte* fish. I sat across from her, ready with all I wanted to say: Somewhere Nadine was floating swollen and gangrenous at the end of a river. Her craziest daughter was dead. My mother could relax at last. But Fay was so busy going over lists and fretting about the snow that there was no opening from which to let the story out, no platform from which to offer up the proof.

And then, as we dipped the last of the fish into horseradish, my mother seemed to notice me for the first time. "My goodness, Janie! I've been so wrapped up in everything for tonight I haven't even taken a good look at you! What's new?"

And what did I answer, me with my well-rehearsed script and a car full of props? Me who had been agonizing for months over this very moment? What did I answer? I answered, "Oh, nothing." Because how could I tell such terrible news and ruin my mother's party while she was so full of worry over dinner and roads. How could I tell her when, for once, she was almost peaceful with the work of this Passover dinner? It would be heartless to ruin her *seder*. I couldn't tell her now.

Then mercifully, the phone rang. Aunt Miriam again. I cleared and washed dishes while my mother wondered out loud if this snow would ever stop.

Fay spent the rest of the day talking to and otherwise fussing over the giant chicken which now browned and bubbled in the oven. Matzoh balls boiled on the stove, *tsimmes* thickened, the house smelled like sweet Jewish wine. My bad news throbbed like a headache, but I ignored it. I gave myself over to my mother's busyness and did whatever she asked without complaining. I arranged the *seder* plate and laid it on the table, prepared the salt water and parsley, polished the special goblet that would be filled for the prophet Elijah.

A series of long-distance phone calls to and from Boston secured the fact that Mickey, Electa, Sima, and Dave would brave the snow and drive to Worcester in one car. Every available ounce of my mother's mental energy was now being spent insuring their safe arrival.

At five-thirty my father arrived home bearing a bouquet of beautiful flowers. I took his coat, and he pecked me on the cheek. "Hello stranger," he said with a smile.

"How are the roads, Mel?"

My father scraped the snow from his feet. "Passable, Fay."

"Only passable? Oh, God, I hope they make it in one piece."

My father handed her the flowers unceremoniously and disappeared.

Aunt Miriam and Uncle Al arrived at six on the button with Grandma Minnie in tow. Miriam handed my mother a Passover sponge cake that was easily sixteen-inches high.

"It's gigantic," my mother exclaimed as she set the cake on a glass plate.

"Bionic," Al said. "Take one bite and two more grow in its place."

I took everyone's coat, and they each kissed me. Minnie pinched my cheek and told me it had been too long since she'd seen me. "You don't hear anything from your sister Nadine?"

A shudder ran through me.

"Ma!" my mother reprimanded from the kitchen, "don't get her started."

I brought the coats into my childhood bedroom and hung them in the closet. I stood in the dark for a minute and closed my eyes. What did my mother mean, don't get me started? Did she have a hunch then of the sorrow I'd bring? I breathed deeply and went back to my family. I made small talk as best I could.

For the next half hour my mother and my Aunt Miriam took turns peering out the window, listening for spinning tires. " I hope they haven't driven off the road," my mother said over and over. Finally, a car door slammed. In no time my sister Electa, her husband and in-laws, were banging at the front door and dripping snow in the vestibule.

"Did you ever see such crazy weather?" my mother asked Sima and Dave Robbins as they pulled off their boots. "I just put all the winter clothes in storage. It never fails."

" I was lucky. Haven't gotten around to changing my snow tires yet." Dave handed my father his coat.

"Like I always say, it pays to procrastinate," my father gave me a wink.

"The table is beautiful, Fay!" Sima exclaimed. "Where did you get such flowers?"

"I picked them myself," my father announced.

"OK, everyone, sit down. Let's get this show on the road." My mother herded us all toward the table. "All you fellas got *yarmelkehs*?" For all her fretting over whether or not Electa would arrive alive, you'd think she had just spent the day with her. She never said, "Hello, how are you?" She just shooed Electa into the dining room with everyone else.

My sister put her arm in mine. "Jane, honey, how are you doing? We haven't heard from you since the wedding."

"I'm OK, Electa," I said in my old zombie voice. If I started talking now, I'd wreck everything.

"You look great," she told me, and held my hand as we sat down.

Finally, we were all huddled around the dining room table. Electa and Mickey still sparkled with newly-wed bliss. My father settled in at the head of the table. My mother hovered but did not land. Numbly, I opened my *haggadah* and waited for the festival to begin.

◊ ◊ ◊

The snow ended, the moon rose full and beautiful. My mother joined us at last and made a *barucha* over the white Passover candles. Then Mickey blessed our first cup of Passover wine.

It was hard to stay separate from the *seder* tonight. Over the years Morningstar *seders* had grown shorter and faster in direct proportion to the children growing older and our family's troubles with Nadine. The Passover story flew by so quickly that if you blinked you often missed your favorite part. The four questions, so vital to the ritual of *Pesach*, were treated like a practical joke on the one who read them—usually me—because the asker was the youngest at the table and the youngest at the table—usually me—was already an adult.

But tonight we had new family. Family brought to us by our savior, Electa. This was our first *Pesach* complete with in-laws, and my mother went all out. Maybe to make up for the wedding fiasco, maybe just because this was always how she did things. The table was laden with Mel's flowers, piled high with matzohs, horseradish, *charoset*, and salt water, all in beautiful dishes that sparkled in the candlelight.

The Robbins family brought respect and seriousness to our *seder*, and also their fine senses of humor. I watched in disbelief as my mother, under the influence of two glasses of wine and Sima's urging, leaned back in her chair and simply relaxed.

Nadine was missing, dead, but for years she had been missing and in a way dead. No one else chose to mention it, so why should I? Still, I sucked on those muddy shoes, that deserted violin, like a sore tooth.

My Uncle Al wisecracked his way through the ceremony. He held up the roasted shank bone. "What did you do, Fay, throw it in the dryer? I never saw such a tiny shank bone in my life."

"If you don't like it, Al, try the *seder* next door."

"What a good idea," he said, but when he made as if to leave, Aunt Miriam pulled him back to his seat.

Electa looked more beautiful than ever, and more remote.

Since her marriage she had developed a fascination for all things domestic. She was entranced with my mother's ability to turn fat into gravy, make red Jell-o look like a delicacy on a bed of leaf lettuce. So when the first half of the *seder* was finished and it was time to serve dinner, Electa disappeared into the kitchen along with Miriam and Fay to learn the secrets of the Jewish wife. With all of them in there, plus Sima, who kept leaping up to help, there was no room in the kitchen for me.

I sat instead with my Grandmother Minnie and the men. The men talked about investments and sports. I poured myself an extra glass of wine and held my grandmother's soft hands. I half listened to the men, but mostly I pushed away images that lodged in my head. Pictures of Nadine upside down in a river; Nadine unidentified in a morgue somewhere; Nadine cut up in pieces and scattered all over some stranger's back forty.

Suddenly my grandmother asked in a whisper, "You really don't know what happened to your sister Nadine?"

I put my arm around her and pretended that I didn't hear.

My mother, my sister, and my aunt burst into the dining room bearing a dinner that rivaled Electa's wedding feast. Golden soup that steamed up from the plates, perfectly browned chicken that fell apart on the fork, *cholent* potatoes and *tsimmes*. Our dishes were filled, then emptied, then cleared and more food appeared. Sponge cake, strawberries, whipped cream, and coffee.

When dinner was finally over, when we were stuffed past the point of decency, we leaned back around the table for the rest of the *seder*—more Passover stories, more wine, plenty of singing. We sang songs I hadn't heard since childhood. Mickey, Dave, and my sister Electa argued with each other animatedly about what it meant to be a Jew in the twentieth century. Sima spoke out strongly for equal rights for the Arabs in Israel, and I sided with her. My Uncle Al fell asleep sitting up at the table, but no one cared. Try as I might, tonight I couldn't dislodge myself from the family picture.

My mother was tipsy. I'd never seen her so happy. She laughed and slapped her sister Miriam on the back. This was the way she might have been at Electa's wedding had Nadine not disrupted it. It was a way Fay aspired to be, but only tonight, with much help from others, could she finally achieve it. This gave me some pleasure, and I finally let Nadine's dead body become unstuck from the river bottom in my mind and float on.

Suddenly Electa shouted, "The *afikomen*! We almost forgot the *afikomen*!"

My father slapped himself on the cheek. "I never hid it!"

"Don't worry, Mel," Mickey said with a glint in his eye, "*I* stole it and hid it myself. So *you* have to find it or nobody else can leave the table."

"That reminds me of a true story," Aunt Miriam began. "You know, Fay was the youngest child in our family. In the old days, my father always hid the *afikomen*. The boys were so fast, neither Fay nor I ever had a chance to find it. Well, I got sick of that, so one year I got it in my head to steal it and hide it myself. Fay sees me, and she's struck with guilt. For me, because I took it, and for her, because she saw me take it. 'Give it back, Miriam, or we'll be killed.' Who'd kill us? 'God'—"

"Oh, Miriam, you're embarrassing me." My mother didn't look embarrassed at all. In fact, she seemed delighted to be the center of attention.

Aunt Miriam continued. "I look her in the eye. She's serious. God is going to come down and kill two little girls for stealing a piece of matzoh? Well . . . I never saw a child cry so hard over a piece of flat bread."

"Did you ransom it or not, Miriam?"

"She gave it back," my mother said, triumphant. "She couldn't stand to see me cry, so she gave it back."

"Ma, you employed those techniques even then?" It felt easy for the first time in my life to make a joke with my mother.

"That's right, Jane. She's had years of practice," Mel said. "That's why you girls have such strong moral fiber."

"All but one," blurted my mother.

We all became tense and quiet, then Aunt Miriam pointed to the silver goblet in the middle of the table. "Time to welcome in Elijah!"

My father peered into the cup. "I think he's been here already."

Minnie gave a wink. " Elijah didn't take a drink from that cup. Me and Jane had a few belts while the rest of you were busy gabbing."

"Stalling, stalling," Mickey said. "But I suppose we can welcome in Elijah. Then Mel Morningstar has got to find the *afikomen* or no one leaves the table."

"Sorry, Mickey, but there's one thing I have to do." I pushed my seat back, but before I actually got up my mother asked, "Where are you going, Janie?"

"I'm opening the door for Elijah." For years this was the only way to get any fresh air during the entire *seder* and for years it was my job.

"I hope he's got snow tires," said Uncle Al, who was suddenly wide awake.

"Jane, you can't open the door," my mother suddenly looked panicked. "Bubby is sitting right in the draft. She'll freeze."

"I'll get her a sweater, Ma. We have to open the door for Elijah."

"It's too cold," argued my mother. "It's just a superstition. There's no such thing as Elijah, otherwise we'd all be in paradise by now."

Just then the door bell rang.

"Fay," Sima Robbins said, "he heard you and he came to tell you different."

Everyone laughed, including my mother who sat back and smiled.

"I'll get it," Electa offered.

I pulled my chair close to the table. My mother sighed. She was calm at this moment, and beautiful. Her eyes glistened from the wine and the company. I was overtaken by a surprising wave of love. "Who is it, Electa?" she called, almost distracted.

"It's the prophet Elijah," Electa called back. There was an edge to her voice, but I chose to ignore it.

"Well, tell him to hurry and save us. We haven't got all day."

Suddenly my mother's mouth fell open, and we all followed her gaze.

There, in front of us, stood my sister Nadine in a pair of baggy pants and an army jacket that was two sizes too big. Her wild hairs flew in every direction. Behind her shuffled the woman who worked at the restaurant in New Chelm, a nervous grin on her face. They were followed in by Electa, who stood behind them glaring, her arms folded tightly across her chest.

"Oh my God," my mother gasped across the silent table.

"Good *yontiff*," Nadine scratched, her head bent a little, but attached to her body, all of her fingers in place. She bowed to my parents. She gave my grandmother a kiss.

"Dolly," my grandmother whispered. Tears welled up in her eyes.

"Good *yontiff*?" my mother was incredulous. "Yes, it was a good *yontiff* until about five minutes ago. What, Nadine, gives you the right to come barging in here like some kind of gangster?"

Aunt Miriam looked at the Robbins family, then at my mother. "Fay, you haven't seen the girl in God knows how long. The least you can offer is something to eat—"

Indeed, Nadine looked ravenous.

"Really, Nadine, sit. You and your friend. What did you say your name was?" Aunt Miriam got up and offered her own chair.

"She didn't say," my mother answered. Her pacific smile became suddenly sinister.

"Oh, Nadine," Aunt Miriam begged, "we have lovely food here! Your mother has been cooking for days—"

"I am not hungry."

My father started stroking his jaw. My sister Electa stood glaring and tapping her foot. I felt caught between fury and relief. At least I now knew Nadine was not dead.

"Well, if you didn't come for dinner, sweetheart," my aunt entreated, "what is it you want?"

"I have come for forgiveness."

"Forgiveness?!" screeched my mother.

Then all hell broke loose.

199

Everyone was shouting at once, except for the Robbins family, whose mouths froze open. My mother's voice rose fiercely to the top of the din and silenced all others.

"So, you want forgiveness." She looked so calm it was frightening. "Now, after months have passed, when I am finally able to forget about you and all the shame you have laid upon me, when I am finally able to relax for ten minutes and have a good time, you come back from whatever rock you crawled under. Now you want to be forgiven?" She slammed her hand down on the table. The dishes shook.

"The shame she laid on you?" Electa yelled. "It was my wedding she terrorized, not yours for God's sake!"

I stood wedged between Electa and my mother, numb with rage. Here was my dead sister, walking and breathing, totally calm. I wanted to kill her.

Then we were all yelling again. My father was pacing in an elliptical pattern behind the table. "I don't believe it, I can't believe it," he said over and over. My mother and Electa railed at Nadine and each other. "Of all the nerve—" one said. "You picked a fine time to show that face of yours," said the other. The shouting filled the house until I could stand it no longer. Something possessed me, perhaps Nadine's *dybbuk*, and I picked up the *seder* plate and smashed it to the floor. It shattered loudly, and everyone was quiet at last.

My mother looked first at me and then at my sister Nadine. "That was my grandmother's *seder* plate!"

Mickey's frozen-mouthed parents looked horrified. Then Sima Robbins leapt to action. She pushed herself up from the table and knelt down over the smashed plate on the floor.

"What does she think she's doing?" my mother muttered.

"If we get all the pieces you can glue it back together. My God, your people brought it all the way from Poland! Don't you want to have something left?"

My Grandmother Minnie shook her head. "Glue it together

with what? Crazy Glue? Let it go, it's old." She sighed heavily and looked away.

Sima took her seat at the table. She piled the rescued pieces neatly before her.

For a long time no one said anything and no one else moved. At last I broke the terrible silence. My voice was solid and fearless. Once I started I couldn't stop. "Welcome home, Nadine! Isn't everyone thrilled to see her? Our prodigal! Our all-time favorite acrobat and disappearing corpse! She's a miracle, everyone. She's Nadine, the Messiah, risen from the dead. And now she wants forgiveness!" Then I swallowed a big gulp of wine from Elijah's cup and sat down with a thump. I felt like a new person.

My mother stood up. She was livid. "We've got two lunatics here. Two crazies! Did I say Nadine had a *dybbuk* in her? *Dybbuk* nothing, she's the devil herself! And Jane is no better—worse even because she at least seems normal. What a matched pair of *vildeh chei-ehs*! And whose womb did they come slithering out of? Who spit them out into the world?" She heaved her thumb at her chest. "Yours truly. Me, Fay Morningstar. I'm the culprit!" Suddenly Fay looked past all of us to Nadine's friend, Rose. "Is that why you came along? To witness this disaster? To make sure we forgave her? We'll forgive her alright!"

Rose giggled a bit in the doorway, but it was a nervous giggle, the giggle of a person trying to disappear. Nadine stood up straight and looked my mother in the eye. "She . . . brought me . . . here."

"What," my mother shrieked, "you didn't fly? I thought you devils only had to close your eyes and be anywhere you wanted."

"Fay, *shah*!" shouted my father.

"I'll *shah* when I want to *shah*!"

Electa put a cigarette between her lips and lit it. She slumped down in her chair and used a saucer for an ashtray.

"That's the *Pesadich* china," Aunt Miriam shuddered. Sima looked, then looked away.

"Animals," my mother shouted, "the whole pack of them is out of their minds!"

Electa looked directly at Nadine and shook her head. Mickey

201

held her hand protectively. "I'm not out of my mind," Electa said, breathing out a cloud of smoke, "I'm furious. Nadine, your timing is perfect. Absolutely perfect. Why the hell did you pick tonight to show up here?"

I held my breath. I knew just what Nadine was going to say. "Why did I come home tonight? Because it is Passover, and this is the night so different from all others."

"A devil!" screamed my mother, "A devil! A devil!"

Before anyone could stop her, Fay Morningstar was slapping her daughter Nadine Pagan on the face with two ferocious hands.

This is how Nadine came back to us from her death and our own. Electa, Rose, and I pulled my mother away from my sister Nadine. Aunt Miriam and Sima Robbins led my mother to her bedroom. She muttered, "Crazy devils, crazy devils," all the way down the hall. Grandma Minnie was quickly bundled up and driven home by Mickey who promised to return. On her way out the door our *bubby* kissed Nadine who said nothing, only shook her head and bit her lips. I sat at the table and fingered the fragments of the *seder* plate I had destroyed. I felt terrible, but strangely free.

My Uncle Al sat at the other end of the dining room table enjoying a cup of coffee and a piece of sponge cake as if nothing strange had happened. My father and Dave Robbins stood at opposite corners of the dining room and stared into space. Electa asked Rose if she would please take Nadine back to wherever they came from. "I don't get you," she told Nadine in full earshot of me and all the men. "It was bad enough you ruined my wedding—I almost *had* forgiven you for that. But this was a special *Pesach*. Mickey brought his family here. Mommy was happy and having fun. This intrusion is unforgivable, Nadine. It cannot be forgiven."

Nadine looked past Electa, past me, toward my father. He shrugged his shoulders and shook his head sadly.

" I wanted to fix it," Nadine said in her gravel voice. My father looked away.

"C'mon, Nadine," Rose said, taking my sister's arm. "It's clear we're not wanted."

Electa looked over at my uncle. She seemed impossibly weary. "How's the cake, Uncle Al?" The question was rhetorical.

Al looked her in the eye and said, "Not bad."

I followed my sister and her friend Rose out the door. The snow was melting already. I was chilly without a jacket. Rose was unlocking her car.

"Wait a minute, Nadine." I wanted to touch her, to talk to her. To tell her how sad it made me to be so angry at her, to assure her that in time I would surely forgive her for being alive. Instead, I opened my trunk and pulled out her violin and shoes. "I have some things of yours, Nadine." My voice sounded stony and cold. She looked at me defiantly, but she came and stood beside me. "These are yours. I found them." I gave her the shoes. Then I held out the violin case. "I'm not sure who this belongs to anymore."

Nadine took the violin case out of my hands. She opened it and examined the instrument closely, plucked a string and held the violin to her ear, ran her fingers over the finish. Held it like a baby in her arms. Then without another word to me, Nadine climbed into Rose's little car and the two of them drove away.

Epilogue

Tikun

In time my mother seemed to forget the wedding disaster, the *seder* debacle. When Nadine's name passed through a conversation, Fay's ears pricked up, her nostrils flared, but then she acted like she'd never really heard it after all. I came home for *Pesach* the next year with a new, silver *seder* plate which we all said we liked, but which really held no candle to our great-grandmother's lovely plate from Poland.

I did not see Nadine again, neither on the streets of New Chelm nor in any form, human or photographic, under the roof of my mother's house. But from time to time, on nights when the moon is full or waning, I have a dream:

> *Nadine and I stand facing each other naked on the top of a mountain in a cave of light. There are women and women around us. Some I know from my life in New Chelm. Others I know from my dreams.*
>
> *A red-headed woman sounds a gong, and we begin to fight. Hand to hand, a wrestling match, two sisters rolling in the moonlight, fighting for our lives, belly to belly, breast to breast, we throw each other off and then pummel each other, tear at each other's skin, our hearts, and then we pull away from each other, only*

205

to fall upon each other again and again, until we are sweating and crying, until one and then the other of us is no longer wrestling, but sobbing and sobbing, holding each other, gasping for air.

"I'm sorry," I tell her, "for all I hoped to be to you, for all I could not be."

"My sister, my true sister," she says in a clear voice. And together we wrestle and weep.

Acknowledgments

Twenty-five years later, I'm still happy to acknowledge the folks and institutions I've mentioned below. In addition, I want to thank the women of Bywater Books: Salem West, Kelly Smith, Marianne K. Martin, and Ann McMan, for their hard work and for seeing lesbian-feminist writing as the essential artistic and political tool it is!

You women rock!

This book was written over ten years in three cities, and would have been impossible to complete without support, criticism, and love from many people. Those people include: Cheryl Muzio, Andi Fiske, Harriet Ellenberger, Catherine Nicholson, Cindy McGowan, Ann Filemyr, and Sebern Fisher who encouraged the earliest tellings of this story; Emma Missouri, Janet Aalfs, Andrea Hairston, James Emery, and Kathryn Kirk who witnessed its Northampton evolutions; Alison Bechdel, Alissa Oppenheimer, Linnea Stenson, Ann Follett, Martha Roth, Perry Tileraas, Alexs Pate, Mary Francois Rockcastle, Louis Alemayehu, and the

Berthas: Barrie Jean Borish, Chris Cinque, Lynette D'Amico, Morgan Grace Willow, Nona Caspers, and Christina Glendenning, all of whom provided community and coaxed me through the Minnesota drafts.

Grace Paley, Len Berkman, and Esther Izbitsky offered continued support and inspiration.

Thanks also to my editor, Nancy K. Bereano, who treats me like a writer; my lover Elissa Raffa, who challenges me artistically, spiritually, and politically; and my friend Susan Denelsbeck, who read and critiqued this book at least five times and accepted only Chinese lunches in return.

I also want to than my parents, Florence and Lester Katz for their generous financial support; the Monkey for Women Fund; the Minnesota State Arts Board; the Loft; the McKnight Foundation; the National Endowment for the Arts; and the Bush Foundation.

Finally, thanks to all the dykes in Northampton, Minneapolis, and points beyond who came to readings, egged me on, and begged for more.

About the Author

Judith Katz is the author of *The Escape Artist* and *Running Fiercely Toward a High Thin Sound*, which won both the Lambda Literary Award and the Crawford Award. She has received Bush Foundation, McKnight Foundation, and National Endowment of the Arts fellowships for fiction; and was the Hadassah Brandeis Scholar in Residence in 2008. She is an academic advisor at the University of Minnesota.

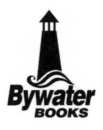

Bywater
BOOKS

At Bywater Books we love good books about
lesbians just like you do, and we're committed
to bringing the best of contemporary lesbian
writing to our avid readers. Our editorial team is
dedicated to finding and developing outstanding
writers who create books you won't want to put
down.

We sponsor the Bywater Prize for Fiction to help
with this quest. Each prizewinner receives $1,000
and publication of their novel. We have already
discovered amazing writers like Jill Malone,
Sally Bellerose, and Hilary Sloin through the
Bywater Prize. Which exciting new writer will
we find next?

For more information about Bywater Books and
the annual Bywater Prize for Fiction, please visit
our website.

www.bywaterbooks.com

www.ingramcontent.com/pod-product-compliance
Lightning Source LLC
Jackson TN
JSHW081329130125
77033JS00014B/463